The smell of the black leopard on the stage
pervaded the room, the essence of the male cat
tingling the senses of the audience. The leopard
had a diamond collar that flashed and glittered
against his ebony coat. The leash that held him
was also jeweled—and at the end of the leash
was the girl, her breathing slow and languorous,
her eyes drugged.

In the darkness Durell saw the prince leaning
forward in his chair, breathing hoarsely.

The music of the flute and drum quickened as
the girl danced around the taut animal, kissing
its head and brow, running her hands down its
strong back. She slid her body along its sleek
flanks, writhing to the beat of the drum. The
audience gasped as the animal swung to the soft
white body and nuzzled the girl, lifting a massive
paw.

Durell moved softly up behind the prince's
chair.

The girl cried out in taunting challenge, strok-
ing the cat, stimulating it to a quick, twitching
frenzy. Someone in the audience moaned. The
drum beat. The tambour rang. The flute wailed.

The curtains at the side of the room stirred,
and two men appeared, holding machine pistols,
heading straight for the prince—and for Sam
Durell.

And the leopard sprang upon the girl. . . .

Fawcett Gold Medal Books
by Edward S. Aarons

Assignment • • • • •

Zoraya

BY EDWARD S. AARONS

A FAWCETT GOLD MEDAL BOOK
Fawcett Publications, Inc., Greenwich, Conn.

Chapter One

It came to Durell in different ways.

It began, in one way, when the aged Imam Yazid Abu al-Maari of Jidrat awoke from a restless sleep and saw the evil shine and glitter of sunlight on the curved dagger blade held between the colonel's neatly manicured fingers.

The Imam was a very old man. And because he had walked hand in hand with death for so very long, he was no longer afraid. He raised himself up on the low bed, among the cushions that supported his frail body, and peered through the ornately carved fretwork of the screening on the balcony. He saw that it was almost time for the noon prayers. There was a white haze over the city. From the height on which Faiz, the imamate palace, was built, he could see Jidrat cupped in the hollow around the crowded harbor with its tankers and dhows and baggalas, all caught forever between burning desert and blazing sea. He saw that Colonel Ta'arife smiled as he sat in the Bombay chair and toyed with his delicate knife.

"Why do you not kill me now?" the Imam asked quietly.

"It is not the time, old man."

"You have overcome the guards, however."

"It was only a matter of silver, Highness."

"If Hamam accepts your bribes, he no longer defends me. Jidrat will soon be yours. You must be ready now."

"Soon," the elegant colonel replied, smiling.

"We are alone?"

"Yes."

"Does the Q'adi Ghezri consent to this?"

"He consents."

The Imam sat. His aged heart beat erratically. Dimly, he could hear the sounds of the city beyond the walls of Faiz, the ancient residence of the feudal rulers of Jidrat. Out in the harbor, the pumps made vague thudding sounds, pouring oil into the tankers that swung at the end of the pipelines —sounds like those of strange animals tethered and sucking at mother's milk. Beyond, the Gulf of Oman was a brazen plate of shining heat.

5

The Imam's room in the palace was lofty and shadowed, cooled by the thick, ancient walls. The tile floor was covered with rugs and carpets. On a taboret inlaid with mother-of-pearl was the Imam's Koran, massively bound in tooled leather. Within the hodge-podge of furniture—Persian cabinets mingling with a modern desk and bookcases—the objects of the old man's true interest were plainly evident. His tired gaze touched lovingly on the volumes of poetry in haphazard collections from Hamasa, Muallaqat, and Mofaddiliyat. The Imam's thoughts wandered slightly, as he recalled snatches of the personal odes of Amru-al-Kais, written fifteen centuries ago. In other collections around the room were the ancient writings of the philosophers, Kindi and Al-Gazel, and the historic works of Bukhari, Ibn Khaldun, and Tabari. In his later years the Imam had devoted himself to resurrecting the golden ages of Arabic literature. Perhaps it was a mistake, he thought now, to have been so unworldly.

Colonel Ali Ta'arife was of the new Arabs—modern, efficient, ambitious, in touch with all the world beyond the shores of Islam. The Imam looked at the colonel's neat, slim figure, the smooth-shaven, angry jaw, the cruel mouth made more cruel by a long and bloody past as chief of police and head of the army of Jidrat. Mockery shone in Ta'arife's dark, intelligent eyes.

The old man sighed. "You are a fool, Ali. You betray your friends for a vainglorious dream. You become a traitor and an eater of camel dung for those who promise much, but who will destroy Islam in the end."

"I work for the greater glory of Islam," Ta'arife replied. "For a rebirth of our holy destiny, Highness. Would you stand against the will of Allah?"

"While I slept, you suborned my guard and entered Faiz like the proverbial serpent," the Imam said. "You may kill me now."

Colonel Ta'arife stared at him. "But where is Zoraya?"

"Lost in the width and depth and breadth of the world."

The Imam found it hard to breathe. His great dark eyes were pools of agony in his eroded face. He was ill. He knew that whatever grew inside him, no matter what the medical hakims said, would never stop growing until he was devoured by it. Ya Allah, it was the will of God, indeed. But, he thought wryly, Allah could have waited just a little longer. There had been so many changes in his lifetime. A man's span of years was like a handful of sand trickling through a jinni's hand. But he had seen his people change from sheepherders living in black tents, smugglers, camel drovers and pirates on the Gulf of Oman, to merchants and world travelers, eventually deteriorating into dissipated roués and fanatic politicians. They had suddenly been thrust, by the discovery of oil, onto the broad stage of the world, like children given a dangerous toy. The new Jidratti were epitomized by the trim, sleek, uniformed Colonel Ta'arife, who sat here with his elegantly polished boots crossed, smiling under his mustache in imitation of the megalomaniac in Cairo.

The Imam looked at his enemy, the colonel. "I worship not that which ye worship," he said softly. "Nor will ye worship that which I worship. To you be your religion, and to me mine."

Ta'arife smiled. "You need not quote the 109th sura to me, Highness. In the Tradition of the Sunna it is also said, 'The difference of opinion in my community is a divine mercy.'"

The Imam felt defeated. He had not expected Ta'arife to be so well acquainted with the moral sayings of Mohammed.

"I must ask you again, Highness," the colonel said. "Where is Zoraya?"

The Imam began to laugh. It was the cackle and wheeze of a senile old man. "Find her," he gasped. "Search the wide world for her.'"

"I must know where she is," the colonel insisted.

"Before you begin?"

"Yes."

"Before you kill me?"

"Perhaps, old man, you will die now."

The Imam shook his head. "No. By the mercy of Allah, it will not be now. You would have killed me in my sleep, otherwise." He could hear, from somewhere in the palace, the monodic music of a nuba, being played upon a long lute. The cantata was both instrumental and vocal, but he could not hear the voice of the singer. He turned back to the colonel. "You do not dare to kill me yet, I see."

"Islam will rise again," Ta'arife retorted. "You, with your old ways, cannot prevent it. The Q'adi will lead all the Arabs in a new and holy jihād."

"I am not that old that I do not know the meaning of war today," the Imam said. "You dream evil dreams. You depend on false friends to supply the arms, yet these same people wait to destroy the Qur'ān itself."

He lay back, gasping. He was an old, old man, his beard was like snow, and the desert had squeezed the juices out of him long ago. Once more he wondered vaguely how Ta'arife had bribed his way past Hamam, the Nubian guard captain, into his sleeping chamber. It did not matter much.

"I will not tell you where to find Zoraya," he said. "She will not help you, even if you do find her. You will have to search the world for her."

"I will find her soon," Ta'arife said darkly. "Then the blood will flow."

It came to Durell in still another way.

It began, too, in the office of U. S. Consul T. P. ("Teepee") Fenner, representative to the independent sultanate of Jidrat, on the Gulf of Oman, an island of desert sand and limestone afloat on a sea of oil, straddling the tanker lanes to the West.

Teepee (Thaddeus Philip) Fenner hated Jidrat. It had been described to him by Senator Henshaw, who had arranged the post for him, as an oasis paradise on the Gulf of Oman. But Fenner hated Jidrat's filth and squalor, hated its oil-wealthy, white-garbed sheiks who drove around in ivory Cadillacs and lived in air-conditioned palaces. He hated the brazen sea, the desert sand, the Arabs, the Imam, the colonel, and the Q'adi. Most of all, he hated his nickname of Teepee, which somehow had followed him here. He did not like to be associated with the Indians of Oklahoma.

He was fat, with high blood pressure, and he suffered from swollen feet in Jidrat's ungodly temperature. He enjoyed only a strain of madness in his essential bigotry.

He was, of course, precisely the wrong man to be posted in Jidrat at this time.

It had seemed right, at first, back in Washington. T. P. Fenner knew the oil business, as only an Oklahoman with wells in his back yard could know it. He'd grown up in the rough-and-tumble days and knew all the tricks of the trade. Never having married, he'd become interested in politics at the state capitol and then in Washington. He was jolly, smart, wealthy enough—so why wouldn't he be at home with the Arabs who suddenly found oil millions pouring into coffers that had previously held only a pittance gained from trade in hides and dates and smuggling slaves across the Rub'al Khali, the Empty Quarter, to the Sauds in Riyadh? It had looked mighty fine to Teepee. It hadn't occurred to him that he could hate the Arabs as much as he hated the Oklahoma Indians who had once sued him for encroaching on tribal lands while in pursuit of oil.

And Jidrat, according to the State Department, was safe, two months ago.

The Imam Yazid Abu al-Maari ruled the small, independent state with an iron, if aged, hand. True, there was the Q'adi, that religious fanatic preaching a new holy war for Islam, reviving not only the Wahabi movement that had put the Sauds into power nearby, but going beyond that into Shiite prophecies that called for a restoration of the true caliphate under an unrecognized Alid imam, who would be known as the Mahdi, the Deliverer. And true, there was Colonel Ta'arife, chief of the army and the police, modeling himself somewhere between Nasser of Egypt and Kassim of Iraq, playing a tortuous game between the Soviets and America, weaving a tapestry of palace intrigue and incipient revolt.

But Teepee could handle it, the State Department had decided.

He hated it. The post as U.S. Consul was not at all the sort of plush, glamorous, powerful job he'd been led to believe it would be.

His office, near the main bazaar, was hot and stifling at the noon hour. He could hear the monotonous voices of praying Moslems in the square, hypnotically repeating the *sikr* in praise of God. He mopped his round, red face with a handkerchief and wished he had stayed at the Hotel al-Zaysir where Messaoud, the bartender, kept a special bottle of Jack Daniels bourbon for him. Instead, he had to deal with this Englishman standing adamantly in his office.

"Goddam it to everlasting hell, Kenton," he said, "but I told you I can't do anything about it! You know the rules here. I can't go running to the Imam and complain that our intelligence man is lost in the desert—"

"Not lost," Kenton said. "I didn't say that."

"No?"

"Murdered."

"What?"

"I saw his body, Mr. Fenner. I want you to see it, too."

Fenner shook his round head. "I've seen dead men before.

This place is built on the bones of dead men. But, by damn, Kenton, you're an Englishman, and it has nothing to do with you! Why not stick to your bones and stones in your digging? Don't come telling the U.S. Consul what to do, damn you!"

The English archeologist was bony and tall, with a long placid face that rebuffed Fenner's words and refused to accept his insults. Paul Kenton was patient. He stood there and stared down at Fenner.

"Blaney was your man. Don't you believe me?"

"I hardly knew him," Fenner replied. "He never came around here. Never told me what he was up to. Had his own office. Far as I'm aware, he was an economic attaché working on the oil contracts for next year. It's you who say he was an intelligence man."

"He told me so," Kenton said quietly. "I believed him."

Fenner sighed. "Well, I'll send a wire home on it."

"Coded, of course."

"Are you still telling me the consulate's business?"

"I want you to see Blaney's body," Kenton insisted. "He was my friend. Esme and I often had him to dinner. He's still out there."

"Why didn't you pick him up, then?"

"I think the Arabs want you to see him, too."

Fenner's mouth fell open. "How do you know?"

"I've been here a long time," the Englishman said. "I'm almost Arab myself. I didn't touch him. I came straight to you."

Fenner chewed his lip. His white drill suit was rumpled, sweat-stained. "What do you think happened? Was it one of the natives running haywire?"

"No. This was slow, bloody, deliberate, and painful."

Reluctantly, Fenner got up. "All right. All right. Let's go see."

Fifteen minutes later they drove out along the new palm-lined boulevard through the Bab-as-Salam, the Gate of Peace, and were on the relatively trackless desert. Five miles from the port of Jidrat, the Englishman indicated a turn off the trail. To the west, the harsh Djebel Haradh Mountains loomed against the brazen sky. The spot might easily have been the moon; there was nothing here but desolation, an emptiness lost in the blinding white haze of the midday heat.

Fenner parked the consulate jeep at the head of a narrow wadi and got out, wincing under the double assault of the sun's heat from above and the reflected heat from the stony

ground below. There was some fresh camel dung beside the
trail that Paul Kenton directed him to follow. He tried not
to breathe too deeply of the fiery air and walked with head
down after Kenton, following a zigzag trail along the floor of
the ravine.

"What were you doing out this way, anyway?" Fenner
asked.

"My diggings are this way. A few miles farther out, at Ain
Gemilha. Astonishing ruins, really. I found a direct connec-
tion between the culture evidenced in the shards and the Nabatean developments in the Sinai and Negev areas."

"What made you stop here?"

"Blaney was still alive. He cried out." Kenton's long,
impassive face suddenly yielded to an intense rage. "Johnny
was dead by the time I'd scrambled over to him. I hope you
have his recent reports. They will be important."

Fenner hesitated, then admitted reluctantly, "All right. I
knew he was a sort of gumshoe. But he always saw spooks.
These Arabs conned him properly. He saw Russians and rebellion everywhere."

"Well, he found some of it, I think. There he is."

The Englishman lifted a hand and pointed.

John Blaney's body was staked and spread-eagled on the
desert flint, naked under the incredible white sun. His mouth
was open: a black hole showing the bloody stump of his
tongue. His eyes had been cut out. There was another bloody
stump below his navel. An intricate pattern of fine, sharp
lines had been carved on the skin of his stomach with the
delicate point of a sharp knife.

T. P. Fenner looked and turned away and his stomach
lurched and he vomited. Finally, he looked again.

"That ain't Blaney," he whispered hoarsely.

"It is."

"But . . . why?" he whispered. He forgot the heat, the silence, the rocky rim of the wadi that closed in upon them like
the fingers of an iron fist. "Why did they do it?"

"He discovered something dangerous, obviously."

"But what?"

"Don't you know?" the Englishman asked. "He worked for
you. You admit now that he was your intelligence man,
right?"

"You're too smart for your own good, professor. Do all
those squiggly cuts on his body mean anything?"

"It's writing. It says, 'Death to the Imperialist Spy.' "

Fenner didn't believe him. He looked again at the mutilated body. He couldn't believe that such savagery still existed. He wanted to throw up again, and his stomach heaved, but there was nothing left of his breakfast in him.

"All right. I'll get off a cable pronto."

The cable went to Washington, and from the Foreign Office of State it was sent to K Section of the CIA. At No. 20 Annapolis Street, the electronic files were checked. There was a conference between General Dickinson McFee, head of K Section, and several Middle East experts. It took place at two o'clock in the morning.

"Jidrat has to stay with us," an anonymous gray-haired man told McFee. "And not just for its oil. It's in a strategic spot, but more important than any possible shipping restrictions, it's a symbol of the whole area since the British gave up there. If we lose the imamate, we'll lose more. You've heard of the Q'adi Mohammed Ghezri?"

"Some sort of religious fanatic," McFee said.

"Right. We can lose the whole Middle East if he gets started."

"I can sent another man out there," McFee said. He looked irritated. It was August, and hot in Washington, and he hated to learn that another man was dead. He had liked Blaney.

The anonymous man had bleak eyes that seemed to be looking deep into destruction. "If we could only get Prince Amr to go back. The Imam is too old, probably senile now. The prince is somewhere in Europe, as usual, drinking, gambling, drugging himself to death. . . . Did you know he went to Yale, Dickinson?"

"No," McFee said. "I can't know everything."

"Things were different then. Yes, he was educated in this country. Amr ibn Alid al-Maari must have made some friends among his American classmates, long ago. What we might do is persuade him to go home to Jidrat and take the reins firmly in hand again. Ram a steel rod up his spine, so to speak."

Someone in the conference muttered, "He's a disgusting swine."

"Granted. But his people would back him up."

"He's a womanizer, a degenerate, a weakling."

"Amr is a symbol of authority that the Jidratti would follow, other than the Q'adi or that Colonel Ta'arife. There's a lad we've got to watch, too. Amr is the only opponent we can put up."

"Didn't he run out on some girl?" asked McFee. "Some desert princess he was supposed to have married as a child?"

"Yes. Zoraya. The scandal sheets ran some stories on it some months ago."

"Didn't she follow him to Europe?"

"Yes, she did. . . . Are you suggesting we persuade her to help us with Amr al-Maari?"

McFee stood up. "I've got a man who may have known your prince when he was at Yale, years ago. A man who might find Zoraya for you, too. His name is Sam Durell."

The Q'adi Ghezri watched the crowd from behind the screens of his balcony. Behind him, the gallery circled an oasis of peace, a garden with a huge bowl, supported by stone lions, in which a fountain swayed and tinkled. In the narrow street below, the crowd of Jidratti listened to the impassioned oration of a street speaker, one of the dedicated workers for the cause. The crowd swayed with the rhythm of a hypnotized cobra, chanting its replies, roaring its approval, screaming with impassioned hatred. The Bombay Hindus whose shops fronted on the street had discreetly put up their iron shutters and closed for the day. Their barasas, the platforms in front of their shops, were empty.

"Al hamdu lillah rab al alimin!" cried the street speaker. "Glory to Allah, Lord of the Two Worlds. If you die martyrs, paradise is your abode, God be praised!"

From the tiled room behind the Q'adi, Colonel Ta'arife spoke gently. "We waste time. As you see, everything is ready."

"Not quite, Colonel."

"The atmosphere will never be more propitious."

"Have you decoded the American's cable?"

"It is done, Q'adi. Nothing will be accomplished there."

"We must make sure of Amr."

"The prince? He is smothered in the soft, perfumed flesh of women. He dreams with the lotus, Q'adi. He is no longer a man."

"The mob down there adores him, Colonel."

"Amr will not return."

"Are you sure?"

"I will make certain."

"The Americans will try to bring the prince back. And possibly with Zoraya. How can you be sure this will not happen?"

Colonel Ta'arife answered, simply, "Death is sure. It is a certainty for all men, Q'adi, even as the Qur'ān promises paradise to all fighters for Islam. And death can be arranged."

The Q'adi was silent, looking down at the dust and heat and confusion of the bazaar below. He was a tall figure in a black robe, with hooded, thoughtful eyes and a long face of strength and intelligence. He was the chief religious judge of Jidrat; his word was the law. He was an expert in interpreting not only the one hundred and fourteen suras, the chapters of revelations in the Koran, but also the Sunna, with its collection of Traditions that contained all the elaborations of Koranic teaching.

Not many people knew of his travels during the years before and after his traditional hadj, the pilgrimage to Mecca where he had bowed in the dust before the Kaaba and recited the long prayers required of every Moslem who hopes to attain heaven.

He had seen the world, and he knew the feel of its substance. He knew that never before in history had opportunity been so finely shaped to the times.

He felt in himself the fervor of his cause and the immutability of his destiny, like a reflection of the heat of the sun on the sea, the light on the desert. It would be as Allah willed. Colonel Ta'arife had his own ambitions; he was akin to those others who came with machinery and promises, with evasive words and propaganda against the Western imperialists. All true, all true. But they were no more to be trusted than the English before them, and the Americans now—those international businessmen who had corrupted the land and the people.

He remembered Jidrat as it was in the old days, when camel caravans filled the bazaar below, when sheep and goats were herded through the narrow streets, when the harbor contained only a few dhows and baggalas, traders and slavers from across the sea, to help the slave market flourish with cheap labor.

Today, there were the big, flashy cars of the tribal sheiks whose lands held oil, who were held in feudal submission to the aged Imam. Today there were both camels and Cadillacs, neon lights on the Mosque of Jidrat, and an electronic voice replaced the muezzin in the minarets for the five daily prayers.

It would all be useful. One bowed to the destiny prescribed by God.

The Q'adi turned and looked at the colonel. "Do you suggest now that Prince Amr be found—and killed?"

"It will be safer." Ta'arife shrugged elegant shoulders. "It can all be arranged. If you insist on waiting until the matter of Zoraya is cleared up, however . . ."

"The woman must not be allowed to interfere."

Ta'arife grinned. "Can she make a corpse walk home?"

"So be it," the Q'adi murmured. He looked back at the cool, remote shadows of his sheltered garden. The water of the fountain splashed and sounded a cooling note against the dry, aching heat of the day. "Kill him, then."

"And the woman?"

"If it is necessary."

"And if the Americans interfere?"

"Eliminate whomever they send."

A roar went up from the crowded bazaar. There were screams and shouts as posters and portraits of the Q'adi and the colonel, all carefully made equal in size, were pushed up and down above the open-mouthed, wild-eyed animal that, with its many heads, was the street mob of Jidrat.

The Q'adi sighed and turned and left the balcony.

In Washington, McFee was on the telephone in his office at No. 20 Annapolis Street. It was a private line with top security restrictions. The man at the other end was never mentioned by name.

"I have the man for you," McFee said. "I was right. Sam Durell is in Geneva at the moment."

"So is the prince. Just coincidence?"

"I sent Durell there yesterday."

"Good, Dickinson. We've checked all the probabilities, as many aspects of the situation as we could. There will be an upset in Jidrat very soon. A matter of days."

"What does T. P. Fenner say?"

"It doesn't matter. We'll leave him there. It will serve as a cover, indicate that we're not aware of what could happen there."

"He can do a lot of harm," McFee said angrily. "How a man like that gets put into a sensitive spot—"

"Let us consider your man, Dickinson. He's been briefed?"

"Not yet. Haggarty is in Geneva. He can do it."

"Good. There's one other thing, Dickinson."

"Yes, sir?"

"Let's try to keep him alive."

Chapter Two

DURELL slept until nine o'clock and then made two telephone calls. One was to the room clerk at the Hotel de la Paix, ordering breakfast; the second was a deliberately dialed wrong number. He sat on the edge of his bed, the spectacular Swiss Alps looming beyond the lake that shone in the distance from his hotel-room window, and listened carefully to the hum, the click, and the slight electronic hesitation when he made the second call. He was certain, as he hung up with apologies in French to the woman who'd answered his wrong number, that his telephone was tapped.

It had been quick, efficient, and ominous. He thought about it for a moment and decided to do nothing about it.

He showered and dressed and ate the breakfast sent up by the management.

It was a warm, sunny day in Geneva. The city was caught in a building boom, jolted out of its medieval, Calvinist atmosphere. You saw Madison Avenue-type Americans—complete with gray flannels, crew cuts, and Ivy League voices—almost as often as you saw native Swiss. Everywhere there were branches of American investment companies, manufacturing corporations, banks, U.S. government departments. The present meeting with the Russians on this neutral ground dealt with the subject of propaganda. Headlines proclaimed it the "Conference on Abatement of Propaganda." Yet the round table was a marvelous sounding board for the daily ideological blasts that the meeting was designed to curb.

He had finished his second cup of coffee and was thinking of London and the routine work he had cleared up there, when the phone rang.

He answered it carefully. It was Haggerty. "Sam?"

"I'm bugged," Durell said.

"Oh, sure. We know that."

"Your man?"

"Hell no. Don't get stacked off, Cajun."

"I have no cover," Durell said. "What am I here for?"

17

"Call this number." Haggarty recited six digits. "It's a pay phone."

"Not from here."

"Of course not. Outside. Make it in ten minutes."

Durell hung up and went out.

He was a careful man. You had to be careful and suspicious—every minute of every day—or you didn't survive, in Durell's business. He had been with K Section for a long time now—since Korea—and before that there had been G2 and the old OSS in Europe and intelligence work for State. He knew the business. And he knew the business had changed him, set him apart, made him different from most men.

If you told Sam Durell he was dedicated to his job, he would have laughed it off. Yet he knew nothing else, and wanted nothing else. His work was enough.

Sometimes he wished he could get out, but the wish was always followed by the corollary that there was no way out. He was a marked man. At No. 2 Dzerzhinski Square, the Moscow headquarters of the MVD, there was a complete, accurate dossier on Samuel Cullen Durell. The dark, shadowy war in which he fought, in which so many friends had died in remote corners of the world, seemed to go on and on. You walked hand in hand with death, wherever you were. It came in dirty ways, usually: a knife in the back in a Hong Kong alley; a garrote on the Marseilles waterfront; a sudden grenade hurled in Algiers; a runaway double-decker red bus in London; or a sudden push from behind as you waited on a platform of the Paris Metro. . . .

You could never be too careful.

Durell was a tall man with thick black hair tinged gray at the temples, a small, neat mustache, and dark blue eyes that changed to black when his Louisiana temper broke through. He had trouble controlling this temper, and he knew his survival depended on its control. He took carefully calculated risks; but there was, also, always the sudden hunch, the instinctual reaction of the gambler, which he had been trained to be. And this was what had helped him when other men had died and failed in their missions.

He wore a dark blue suit of medium weight, a little too warm for Geneva in August. His white shirt and dark-maroon necktie were inconspicuous. He did not look like either a businessman or a tourist. He moved gracefully; he had trained himself, during endless and tortuous hours of practice, to react instantly. He knew every dirty trick of judo fighting: how to kill a man with a knife, a gun, a thumb, a rolled-up newspaper. And some of this showed in the way he walked and the way he looked at the world.

Long ago, as a boy in Bayou Peche Rouge, down in the bayou country below New Orleans, he'd sat in a pirogue with his old grandfather Jonathan, fishing in the shade of towering old gum and cypress trees that grew along the ancient chenières, and there he had learned the art of hunting and gambling.

The old man—in his nineties now—had been a good tutor. Old Jonathan had been among the last of the old-time Mississippi riverboat gamblers; a man with shoulders and back as straight as a ramrod, with keen eyes and a unique way of looking at the world. Durell's earliest memories were of the old side-wheeler steamer, the *Trois Belles*, on the mudbank near Peche Rouge. The side-wheeler had been home to him after his parents died and he went to live with the strange old man in the bayous.

Old Jonathan had taught him tricks with cards, dice, guns, and knives. The old man knew what it meant to fight for survival.

He was being followed. There was a team of two assigned to him, and the first, a stout Swiss man with a florid face under a ridiculously squared Homburg, picked him up as he left the lobby of the Hotel de la Paix. The second team member was a woman who looked like a young matron on a casual shopping tour of Geneva's downtown streets.

Durell walked along the quai beside the Rhône, heading for the Auberge à la Mère Royaume. It was ten minutes past twelve. The river flowed busily into the broad, bright reach of Lake Geneva where Mont Blanc towered into the blue summer sky, its snow-capped peak dazzling in the sunlight. He wished he had time for an apéritif near the Jet d'Eau, that spectacular hundred-foot fountain spurting from the surface of the lake. Pleasure boats and water taxis hummed on the river. The bridges to the old part of town were crowded with traffic. When he saw he could not shake either tail without being overt about it, he ignored both the fat man and the casual woman and entered a public phone booth on a side street off the Rue du Rhône, near the main shopping center.

He dialed the six-digit number Haggarty had given him, and his call was picked up at once.

"Sam?"

"I'm being tailed. What gives?"

"I don't know. What were you doing in London, Cajun?"

"Nothing vital. Who's your opposite number here?"

"Kolia Mikelnikov. The major of Budapest fame, remember? He's in charge of Russian security at the C.A.P."

"Well, he put two people on me," Durell said. "Maybe they picked me up at the airport. Or maybe you have a leak."

"Either is possible," Haggarty admitted. "No man is infallible."

"Shall I let them ride?"

"Better shake 'em, Sam. Let's meet at Georgi's. Remember it?"

"At the foot of Grande Rue, down in the old town," Durell said. "Near where Rousseau was born."

"You remember the damnedest things about places. In an hour?"

"Time enough."

"Oh, and one thing, Cajun. This job is urgent."

"What job isn't?" Durell asked.

He hung up and stared blankly at the telephone. Traffic bustled outside and he looked at the crowded sidewalk, the busy, clanging streetcars, the beetle-like European autos. Geneva was supposed to be neutral ground; the Swiss were adamant about that. He wondered if the Swiss police themselves had put the fat man and the woman shopper on his tail. Not impossible. But not very likely, either.

He could not see either the Homburg or the matron anywhere.

And then he heard the roar of the approaching lorry. Through the glass of the phone booth he saw pedestrians swirling in from the Rue du Rhône under a bright traffic light. Then he saw the truck. It was American; a converted Army tractor that violated traffic rules by being on this street at all. It came around the corner fast, like a huge prehistoric monster shouldering aside a swarm of unimportant creatures on its flanks.

A woman screamed.

And Durell saw that the truck was headed straight for his telephone booth.

His reaction was instantaneous, a conditioned reflex. He

elbowed the booth door open and spun around to face away from the truck. For one split-second of eternity he thought he couldn't make it, thought this was his moment of fatal carelessness. Then he stumbled to the curb, the roar of the careening truck thundering in his ears. He could see it, out of the corner of his eye, looking like a monster of red steel with a blinding windshield that reflected a stray shaft of afternoon sunlight and effectively erased any glimpse of the driver. Then he dove off the sidewalk and into the street, and from behind him there came a crash of splintering aluminum and glass as the booth was swiped by the truck and hurled into the air. Something struck his shoulder, spinning him around. Something else slammed his thigh. Wheels whined and screamed and he knew he was on his hands and knees in the gutter, traffic shattering its pattern to protect him.

The roar of the truck faded away with remarkable speed and was replaced by the shrieking cry of a woman again and the clamor of angry Swiss voices and the skirl of a police whistle.

"Are you hurt, m'sieu?" someone asked in French.

Durell looked up at a stranger's concerned face. "No. No, thank you."

"You must remain absolutely still. It is incredible. It could have been a terrible tragedy. These American drivers are maniacs."

"I'm all right," Durell said. He knew the driver had not been an American. He climbed to his feet. His legs ached and trembled. He brushed at his clothing automatically. "Quite all right. Thank you. Then you must have seen the truck."

"It is gone, m'sieu. Like the telephone booth. Had you not jumped out at just the right instant, I shudder to think of the ending for you."

Durell saw a traffic cop shouldering authoritatively through the crowd. He could not remain here as the center of attraction. The accident was not an accident at all, of course. It was an attempt on his life, and he could only conclude that Major Kolia Mikelnikov had decided to violate Swiss neutrality in an attempt to eliminate him. But why? What was so special about him now?

Mikelnikov, however, in Durell's book, was something special.

Just as there was a dossier in the MVD files in Moscow

on Samuel Cullen Durell, so there was a similar file on Major
Kolia Vassilivich Mikelnikov at No. 20 Annapolis Street in
Washington.

Major Mikelnikov had gone into Budapest with the Soviet
forces during the Hungarian uprising. He had been associated
with the bloody purges that followed, and Durell, who had
been on a brief mission in the country at that time, had become his prime target. Mikelnikov's assignment contained
orders not to relent until his mission was accomplished. Durell had stung the opposition badly during his brief stay in
Budapest during the turmoil. The result was Mikelnikov's
mission:

Find Durell. Remove him. Destroy him. Eliminate
him. Close the file on Sam Durell.

Chapter Three

MIKELNIKOV had pale blue eyes and a wide mouth and deep seams in the rough skin around his lips. His hair was grayish, cropped close to his well-shaped head. He looked out of place among the tourists crowding the café tables of the Auberge à la Mère Royaume. Yet there was an arrogance, a flamboyant air about the man. You looked at him twice, instinctively. If you met his pale gray eyes, you usually looked away quickly, somehow disturbed by the glimpse of a cold, icy hell. Mikelnikov did not like people studying him, although in his dossier there was a brief note about a short turn in the Bolshoi Theater, where the man had been an actor in his younger years.

There were three other chairs at Mikelnikov's table. A heavy-set man sat on one, talking urgently to the major, who seemed not to be listening. Durell walked angrily toward the table, threading his way through knots of tourists chattering in the sunshine. Pigeons suddenly wheeled and swooped and settled on the sidewalk, coming in from the riverside quai, and then took off again with a great flapping of wings. Durell pulled out a chair at Mikelnikov's table and sat down.

"Good afternoon, Kolia Vassilivich," he said in Russian.

Mikelnikov looked at him and flicked a finger at the heavy-set man. The other man got up clumsily and walked away. Mikelnikov smiled. "Sam, my friend. Gospodin Durell. I heard you were in Geneva this morning, when you arrived by Swiss-air from London. You find the weather here in Switzerland more pleasant?"

"Neutral air is sometimes easier to breathe—if neutrality is respected."

"The Swiss are not always alert to breaches of neutrality. You maintain your CIA drop, run by Mr. Haggarty, for example."

Durell said, "Your truck missed me, Kolia. It was very clumsy, not worthy of you."

Mikelnikov smiled. He had big teeth, one of which was capped with gleaming steel. He looked like a bemused horse. "My truck?"

"We can be honest with each other here, Kolia."

"You are angry. It is your Southern temper, perhaps."

"Perhaps. But never too angry, Kolia. I am surprised, and a little concerned about you. You have been on the job over a year. Your superiors must be impatient now. Perhaps there is pressure on you to conclude your business with me."

"It will be concluded," Mikelnikov said. "It is strange, you know. I have come to respect and admire you, Durell. I wish you and I could be friends."

Durell waited.

"We could make a marvelous team, you and I," Mikelnikov added, "if we combined our talents in our profession."

"Are you suggesting you may defect and come over to our side?"

Mikelnikov laughed. It was a braying sound, harshly disturbing over the muted chatter of the tourists at adjacent tables. "You could come over to us, gospodin."

"I wouldn't be happy at No. 2 Dzerzhinski Square," Durell said. "An organization that commemorates the name of Feliks Dzerzhinski is not for me. Surely you know that this Pole, although a Bolshevik of the old school, was the bloodiest butcher of all. Look at the record: the first secret police chief of the Cheka; a ghoul; a mass murderer. And from the Cheka came the OGPU and the NKVD under Stalin, and now the MVD. Do you really know Dzerzhinski's record? Do you know what he did to the peasants in the Minsk area, in the Ukraine—"

"Enough." Mikelnikov held up a big, rough hand. He was not smiling. "It is simply a matter of viewpoint. We cannot meet, I see."

"No."

"You will never join us?"

"You know that is a stupid question."

"But I do not really wish to kill you."

"You won't," Durell said.

"Yes, I will. I must. And it will be done soon."

"Are you warning me now?"

Mikelnikov drummed thick fingers on the table. His fondue was untouched. Under his shaggy brows, the bony ridges seemed doubly heavy, and there were deep hollows in his cheeks. For just an instant he looked haunted and trapped. But he was no less dangerous than before. Perhaps more so, Durell thought.

"You may call it a warning, Durell. Go back to London. Your assignment here in Geneva is an empty and hopeless mission."

"What would you know about it?" Durell asked.

"You will be briefed by Haggarty this afternoon, I assume. And then you will leave. But I suggest that you decline the job. It will mean your death. I guarantee it."

"Those are your orders?"

"Yes."

"Yet you tell me about them?"

"As I said, I respect and admire you. We could be friends."

"They will shoot you if they learn of your affection," Durell said dryly.

"Who will tell them in Moscow?" Mikelnikov leaned forward earnestly. "If I weep for you one day, Sam Durell, it will be tears I shed alone. I am not ashamed of tears. We understand each other. We have been enemies so long that in a sense we are true friends. . . . Were you a good friend of John Blaney's?"

"Blaney?"

"Please. You knew him. He was recently assigned to the Middle East—to Jidrat. An intelligence officer for your consul there, Mr. T. P. Fenner."

"Do you expect me to applaud your information?"

"No. You know as much about us, or more. But Blaney is dead. And you will be sent to Jidrat to replace him."

Durell's face was blank. He gave nothing away. But for the first time he felt a sudden uneasiness, an awareness of danger perhaps of the worst sort . . . perhaps the ultimate danger, after all.

"So you sent the truck to kill me?"

"Yes. I know it will not stop you," Mikelnikov said. "And I shall wait for you one day, somewhere. I shall wait, Durell."

"Your bosses must consider my job important."

"We agree on that." Mikelnikov's pale gray eyes were now cold under his shaggy brows, like two stones set in his peasant's face. "Please, my friend, go back to London. Reject the assignment. You can surely do that."

"Not now."

"Tell Haggarty you cannot go to Jidrat. Do not go."

Durell stood up. "Like you, Kolia Vassilivich, I shall miss you when you are removed from the field. I thank you for

warning me. It was unnecessary. I will go to Jidrat. You won't
stop me or kill me."

"I am sorry, my friend," Mikelnikov murmured.

"We are not friends," Durell said.

Mikelnikov watched the tall figure move away through the
crowds on the Rue Saint-Corps. He was conscious of his
own conflicting thoughts. Images of Budapest, almost forgotten, returned unsummoned to his mind. What had happened there, the blood and the torture, was a historical necessity. But he couldn't keep it on an impersonal plane. His own
part in it had been too vivid, destroying his objectivity.

It was Naomi, of course. Her loss was still an unhealed
wound because he did not know what had happened to her.
If she was dead because of the orders he'd had to carry out—
like his orders to eliminate Durell—well, then he would know
how to finish it. But he knew nothing, which was ironic since
it was his business to know everything. To lose one's wife,
and to know no peace thereafter, because one obeyed orders
—as one obeyed this order about Durell—was worse torture
than any carried out on the Budapest prisoners. They, at least,
knew their fate.

His memory of Naomi filled him quietly. She had hated
him at first for what he represented. And then she had loved
him. And, at the end, she had hated him again. A full cycle.
He admired Durell and wished he could know him as a
friend. But it was impossible.

And where was Naomi now? Wandering lost and homeless
in the world? He did not know. When he had gone to save
her from the fury and destruction meted out to others, she
had vanished.

Mikelnikov shook himself mentally. His eyes again saw the
Swiss café where he sat, the bright sunlight, the passers-by.

Durell was gone.

Durell walked to the river and turned back at the bridge
over the Rhône. Mont Blanc was touched by white fire on
its peak. He turned right on the Rue du Rhône and, in a
small restaurant, stepped into another phone booth and
dialed a number—22-04-32. Presently he spoke to Haggarty.

"Yes, it's important, Cajun. I heard about the truck."

"Your security is rotten," Durell said. "I've just had a
talk with Major Mikelnikov."

"Cajun, don't beg for it. You're due at Georgi's."

"Just wanted to let you know I'll be there."

Haggarty chuckled. "I've already received a report on your date with the major, Cajun. Am I supposed to be upset, because you fraternize with the enemy?"

"All right, Hag. I'm not in the mood."

"Sorry. See you—I hope."

Durell used various evasive tactics to make sure he was not being followed. They were time consuming, and tedious, but within twenty minutes he was reasonably sure he was alone as he walked by the thirteenth-century Tour de l'Ile and then turned down through the foot of the Bastions into the old quarter. Georgi's was at the foot of the Grande Rue, the oldest street in the old town, near where Rousseau was born and where Calvin once preached his doctrines. Haggarty was waiting there.

The café was small and had tiled walls, a bar, and booths. It was not crowded. Haggarty sat with his back against the tiled wall. He pulled out a chair as Durell approached, and watched the entrance.

"Hello, Sam."

Durell nodded. "Do you have a man outside?"

"Two of them. We're all right here." Haggarty grinned. "I know how you hate organizational mumbo jumbo, Cajun. But contain yourself. You'll be off on a lone-wolf project soon enough."

"Does anyone tell me about it? Or do I wait for Mikelnikov to read me my assignment?"

"Take it easy, Cajun. We do the best we can."

"It's not good enough, if people get killed."

Haggarty frowned. He was a thin, nervous man with a habit of blinking his eyes as if he perpetually had dust in them. He had a hot chocolate in front of him on the round table.

Durell knew he was being unnecessarily sharp with Haggarty. He didn't have to tell Haggarty that care was needed to stay alive in this business. He paused and lit a cigarette, and surveyed the café. It was a workingman's place, innocuous, off the tourist beat. You look over your shoulder, he thought, and under the bed and behind the wallpaper, and then you do it all over again, and then you count ten and wonder what you missed.

He said, "I'm surprised to find you my contact, Hag. Your division has always been the Middle East. Geneva is a long way from Cairo, Tel Aviv, or Baghdad."

"And Jidrat. Lately I've been in Jidrat. Know it, Cajun?"

"Mikelnikov mentioned it, and said that John Blaney is dead. Were you there when it happened?"

"I passed through, on a scream for help from the fathead we've got there as consul. Teepee Fenner, the great Oklahoma Okie. I couldn't do anything."

"I've never been there," Durell said, "but I know it's one of those wealthy, independent sultanates built on oil—paternalistic, feudal, and savage. A hell-hole where you think it's cool when the temperature drops to one-twenty in the shade. It's a long way from Geneva."

"Not as far as you think," Haggarty said. "I wanted to stay on in Jidrat, but they pulled me off it to meet you here. I'm on my way home to New York." He blinked again, sipped at his chocolate, and when he returned the cup to its saucer, the blue china made a faint rattling sound. He rubbed two fingers across his mouth. He had a small, sandy Arabic beard. His skin was burned a dark bronze color in which his eyes, which were the color of the blue cup, seemed to contain a blind blue pallor.

Durell hid his sense of disturbance. He knew Haggarty casually, from past meetings in far corners of the world.

Haggarty went on apologetically. "I'm not good enough to take on Jidrat, apparently. Fenner down there has some powerful connections. But he's a bungler, Sam. He can get you killed."

"If I go there, I'll be careful."

"Yes. You'll go. And I'm on my way home to the States. To a desk job in computation, analysis, and synthesis."

"That's important, too," Durell said. "You add up the bits and pieces and construct a picture for the Joint Chiefs, the Pentagon, the White House, and the National Security people."

"I know, I know," Haggarty said impatiently. "All the same, I goofed. You don't get switched on an assignment just after you start, otherwise. Maybe I was too anxious to find out about John Blaney. You see, we were good friends. He died hard, Cajun."

"We all do," Durell said.

Haggarty breathed heavily. "I keep thinking of how Fenner described Blaney's death, and I know I'm no good any more. I hope you've kept up with your Arabic, Sam."

"I have. Do you brief me, or am I left to guess my way into this? From what I've read, Jidrat is a tight spot these days. Between that religious fanatic, the Q'adi, and Colonel Ta'arife, who'd like to imitate Nasser or Kassim—nobody knows which one, and maybe he doesn't know himself—and the old Imam, who's quite a respectable literary figure, incidentally—well, something has got to boil over. It's becoming obvious. And the old Imam can't stop it, right? If we could get Bogo back in line, though—"

"Who?" Haggarty asked.

"Prince Amr al-Maari. The next in line to rule. After the Imam."

"Bogo?"

"We called him that at Yale," Durell said. Then he looked at Haggarty and nodded. "It adds up, Hag. That's why they want me. Because I knew Bogo at Yale. Years ago, when the old Imam sent him to America for a touch of Western culture."

"Yes, it adds up. They'd have that in your dossier at K Section," Haggarty said. "That's why you're so special."

"It's in my dossier at MVD headquarters, too," Durell said wryly. He sat back and added, "But it's a long shot."

"Have you been in contact with the prince since Yale days?"

"No."

"Washington still thinks you can influence him, though."

"I suppose that's it," Durell said. "Where is he?"

"Here, until last night, that is. In Geneva."

"So that ties Jidrat to Geneva."

"Right."

"What am I supposed to do?" Durell asked. "I knew Amr al-Maari when he was one-and-twenty. We called him Bogo, sure, but I can't even remember why. And I haven't seen him since."

Haggarty looked grim. "He's no schoolboy now. I've checked his career since he took over his private oil farm—when his father was assassinated and his brother killed in a tribal feud. Your friend Bogo got bored with it all and left the reins in his grandfather's hands—the old Imam—and he's been out-doing Farouk seven ways from Sunday ever since."

Durell nodded. "He was a nice, shy kid at Yale, when I knew him."

"Well, he grew up fast. You've read about him in the Sunday supplements—dope, vice parties, the orgies at his place on the Riviera, his regular bouts in Swiss sanatoriums to wring himself out. That's where he is now—or was. At the Hospital St. Homerius, out of town."

"You don't think he's still there now?"

"Nobody can get to see him. That's why we're not sure." Haggarty touched his wispy Arabic beard. He looked haunted. "I wish we could get Fenner out of Jidrat. But somebody loves that fat little bastard. He's in the sands of Jidrat up to his neck; moored there forever, it seems. It'll take more than a mere agent like me to yank him out."

Durell persisted. "You haven't said what I'm to do."

"You've got to put some steel into your pal Bogo's spine. Ram it up his rear end and make him walk like a man, go home, and straighten things out. According to the extrapolations of State and Pentagon, if Jidrat goes flaming nationalist 'neutral' like Cairo, or if this Q'adi takes off on a holy jihad, warring against all Western unbelievers like the old Moslem Brotherhood, we're in the soup.

"That's what the computing machines say. That's what common sense says, too. In Jidrat, you've got the worst sort of paternalism added to the wildest brand of Arab nationalism. And it's mixed with that peculiar savagery the Arabs seem to specialize in. The place is in ferment—a microcosm of the whole world in this one Arab sultanate. Mud shacks and starvation and goats and camels next to air-conditioned palaces, foreign sport cars, and polo ponies. The old Imam can't hold out much longer. The Q'adi and our two-bit Hitler, Colonel Ta'arife, have temporarily allied themselves to get rid of the old man and take over. And the only one who can pull the country together is Prince Amr al-Maari, the playboy of the world."

"He may not even remember me," Durell mused.

"Well, if you can get him to go back home like a man, things will calm down. The Jidratti are devoted to him. But it has to be done fast, Cajun. Before the lid blows off. And he doesn't want to go home." Haggarty grunted. "I can't say I blame the son of a bitch. But it will be your job to persuade him, Sam. Remind him of joyous college days and all that. And Zoraya."

"Zoraya?"

"She's in your file, too. The prince's betrothed. Some say he married her when she was just a child—and he won't go near her. We can reach Zoraya, though. We found her hiding out in Elba. Living on hope, I guess. Loving that bastard and constantly being slapped down by him. Yet he listens to her, it seems. You knew her, didn't you?"

"She was just a child," Durell said, frowning in the effort to remember. "There was one time, in Baltimore, when I went with Bogo to see her . . ."

"Use her, if you can. We've contacted her. She remembers you, Cajun. She'll see you." Haggarty looked exhausted. "It's up to you to work it out. I'm just handing you the pieces. It's up to you to make a man out of the worst bum in the world and get him to go home and run things right. Use the girl if you can. Use the prince. But don't waste any time."

"All right," Durell said.

"And you've got one other job you can do for me, Cajun."

"Yes?"

"You can find out who killed John Blaney."

Chapter Four

DURELL walked back through the old quarter of Geneva to his hotel. He thought about Bogo, Prince Amr ibn Alid al-Maari of Jidrat. An educated savage with a prep-school accent acquired after four years at Yale. A small man with a feline face and flashing teeth and an arrogant manner with money. An arrogant manner with people, too, on those occasions when he noticed them at all. An inhuman contempt that placed a negligible value on those things that ordinary mortals considered important and essential.

The slim Arab boy had somehow taken to Samuel Cullen Durell, grandson of a Mississippi river gambler. Durell remembered how, in his junior year, the money had stopped coming from Bayou Peche Rouge, for some obscure reason, and he'd gone to MacTivers in East Haven to become a dealer for MacTivers in the gambling games there. Old Jonathan had taught him well; Durell was the best dealer MacTivers had ever seen. Still only a schoolboy, Durell even then could weigh risks with a gambler's careful estimate. He'd made a lot of money for MacTivers. If the Yale authorities had ever learned about his extra-curricular job, he'd have been thrown out of the University, of course. But they'd never heard of it.

Amr al-Maari had come to MacTivers' joint with some upper-classmen who fawned on the prince for his wealth, enjoying the use of Amr's convertible and free money. The prince had already been initiated into the mysteries of poker by classmates in the dorm, but MacTivers' place was professional, the game was fast and hard and ruthless, and he was faced with experts.

In twenty minutes the prince lost six thousand dollars. His manner of playing was not subject to advice.

The prince was a poor loser, Durell remembered, and he recalled the thin fox face, the dark, frustrated congestion of blood in the sallow cheeks. Amr al-Maari had been pampered all his life, allowed to win at his games by the sycophants around him.

But Durell had no pity. He needed the dealer's job. He

could have cheated, of course. His fingers were supple and deceptive. He knew every trick in the book, taught to him by old Jonathan on long, hot afternoons aboard the wreck of the *Trois Belles* moored in the bayou below Peche Rouge. Mac-Tivers wanted Durell to use those tricks, and he thought Durell had worked the cards to take Amr for the first six thousand. But this wasn't true. The prince was simply a poor poker player with an appalling disregard for the value of money.

Nevertheless, Amr's anger boiled over at last.

In the quiet room with its green octagonal table where the harsh cone of light spilled over chips and cards and gamblers' hands flickering in and out on the play, Amr al-Maari suddenly leaped to his feet with a shrill, thin curse in Arabic.

"You cheat me! I will cut out your heart!"

And, astonishingly, there was a knife in Amr's thin hand, a slim, curved blade with an ornate, jeweled handle. The steel flickered wickedly in the cone of smoky light over the table. Everything seemed to explode: chips, cards, thick bodies all tumbling out of the way.

Only Durell sat still, facing the danger.

He looked up at the congested face and the knife-point at his throat. He kept his hands in plain sight, flat on the table.

"I did not cheat you, Bogo."

"You lie! It must be so. I never lose."

"That's because your friends see to that," Durell said.

"Eh? What do you say?"

"You're a rotten poker player. You shouldn't be allowed near a professional table until you've learned the rules of the game."

"No one speaks to Amr like this!" the boy shrieked.

"I do. I will. If nobody else will tell you the truth, I will, Bogo. Now put that knife away."

There was a moment's pause. The Arab's body trembled in the storm of his passion. Yet the knife was held steady. Durell knew he was very close to death.

Then Amr whispered, "You are not afraid?"

"Of course. Only a fool is not afraid."

"Yet you sit here and tell me I am a poor player? You dare to insult me?"

"It was not meant as an insult. Only as advice. And the truth."

"You did not cheat? On your honor?"

"On my honor."

The fox face grinned cruelly. "I could kill you, anyway. I would not be punished for it. No. I am too important to your government. They would find an excuse for me. They would call it a schoolboy prank."

Durell's voice hardened. "Put that knife away, Bogo."

"You speak as if you give me orders."

"I do. I've had enough, Bogo. Put it away, sit down, and play cards. Or get out."

MacTivers' voice rumbled out of the smoky background.

"God, boy, be careful. He's a savage in schoolboy pants—"

Durell moved. His hands were quick, flickering, strong. The edge of his palm cracked against Amr's wrist in a slashing blow. Old Jonathan had taught him what to do against a man armed with a knife. Durell was fast and accurate. The blade went spinning to the table, shone evilly on the green baize. Durell swept it to the floor and stamped on it, broke it. And stood before the Arab prince.

"I'm sorry, Bogo. I've had enough of you."

Amr ibn Alid al-Maari breathed deeply. His eyes flared. He hated Durell. And then something changed in him. He shook his head. He picked up the pieces of the knife. He began to laugh softly and said something in Arabic that Durell, at that time, could not understand.

"We will be friends," said the Prince of Jidrat.

Durell reached the Hotel de la Paix without incident. No one followed him. The desk clerk had an envelope for him. He waited until he was alone in his room before he opened it. Inside the envelope was four thousand dollars in American currency and a series of airline tickets to Rome, Athens, Ankara, and Jidrat. There was no message, but none was needed. He knew the envelope had come from Haggarty.

At five o'clock he got his rented Fiat from the garage and drove out along the lakeside highway toward Lausanne, following the northern shore of Lake Geneva. The city already exhibited its flare for notorious night life. The Genevese, Durell thought, originally reared in the traditions of John Calvin, whose pulpit still stood in St. Peter's Cathedral, had come a long way from the Protestant sumptuary laws. He drove past ornate villas and the vast, mausoleum-like piles of League of Nations' buildings. His thoughts swung back to Bogo and a frightened girl named Zoraya.

He had first met Zoraya on that night when Amr had come to the room near MacTivers' place where Durell lived during his undergraduate days. Amr had been upset. His thin, arrogant face had been perspired although the October New England day had been raw and bleak.

"Sam? Cajun? Can you come with me?"

"Where?" Durell asked. It was late in the evening and he had been reading law and thinking of bed. "What's the trouble?"

"I must go to Baltimore."

"Baltimore? Now?"

"I must get a look at her."

"At who? What are you talking about?"

The prince explained impatiently. The Imam Yazid Abu al-Maari, his grandfather, had sent him orders. He was to visit Zoraya, the daughter of a powerful sheik—a man educated in England. Zoraya's mother had been English. In any case, it was part of the Imam's old feudal policy of arranging political matches this way, Bogo said. His eyes were shifty. Durell did not think he was getting the whole story.

"Of course," Amr said, "I can have four wives, and concubines if I wish, later on."

"Lucky you," Durell said. "Will you marry this Zoraya?"

"I must see her. I must obey. Will you drive down to Baltimore with me?"

"What about classes tomorrow?"

"Don't worry," Amr said. "I'll fix it."

Durell did not doubt that he could. He went with the slim Arab because Bogo seemed to need a friend, and because, for all the youth's bravado, it was plain that he was frightened, even desperate.

They were in Baltimore an hour before dawn. Near a private school for girls that was surrounded by a high stone wall. The driveway ended in an ornate iron gate that seemed insurmountable in the moonlight. Beyond the shrubbery Durell glimpsed, from the car, a wide sweep of lawn and the blind eyes of ivied windows. The place seemed to be impregnable. There was a brass plate with the name of the school, but it was in the shadows and he could not make it out. He watched Bogo get out of the car.

"What do you do now?"

"We wait," Amr whispered. "Someone will bring her."

"Just what do you expect to do, anyway?"

"Talk to her. See what she is like."

"Do you have any choice in the matter? I mean about marrying her, Bogo?"

"Not now. But I shall. The Imam Yazid rules, at the moment. I am considered only a boy, a schoolboy. But I will not have my choice of brides dictated to me!" Amr spoke with abrupt ferocity.

"She might be pretty."

"I am not concerned with that."

"And intelligent."

"One does not seek a mind in a woman, my friend."

So they waited.

The prince paced up and down the road in the growing, brightening dawnlight.

At last he spoke again. "There. The slave brings her."

"The *slave?*" Durell asked.

"Do not be shocked. We have slavery in my country. All correct and legal—in the order of things—according to the Qur'ān and the Prophet."

There were two figures hurrying toward them. Women who were veiled and muffled, looking odd, somehow, in their Western-style coats in the chill of the October morning. Durell, in his role of spectator and companion to the prince, could only watch with curiosity. His attention centered on the slight figure beside the hulking woman. He was undoubtedly shocked. He was aware of enormous frightened eyes, upon him. And he had a feeling that this was only a child, not more than twelve, playing the role of a woman.

There were mutterings in Arabic; the tones of a quarrel; a sharp haughtiness in Amr's manner as he addressed the woman attendant. She seemed reluctant to agree but terrified to cross the prince's wishes. Durell wondered how Amr had arranged this clandestine meeting in the first place, and then he remembered Bogo's imperious way with people and money. He was not surprised when the older woman fell back and the slight, fearful girl stepped into the car.

"Get in," Amr said in English. "Please drive, Sam."

"Where?"

"Anywhere. I must talk to her."

"This is a hell of a way to arrange a date," Durell said.

"But I must learn what she knows about the Imam Yazid. There is treachery here, I think, and I would not like to be the last to know about it, while I am in this country, playing at being a schoolboy."

Thinking about it as he drove along the shore of the Lake of Geneva years later, Durell remembered that those were the days just before Hitler's war on mankind, when Middle East intrigue still had a flavor or romance and faraway mystery remote from the ordinary world of a Yale man.

The girl had been submissive. He had never succeeded in erasing her from his mind. Most of all, he had been impressed by her enormous liquid eyes, her small face, her humble manner that somehow held a tiny spark of freedom and individual identity.

Durell had driven aimlessly toward the Chesapeake shore that, in later years, during his work in Washington, he came to know so well. At Prince John he found a lane that led to the water's edge and he parked there, somewhat amused by his role as chauffeur, wishing he could understand the mutterings in Arabic that came from the back seat.

The girl's voice was thin, like a flute; anxious at first, almost inaudible, then rising in surprise and anger. Then she was silent for a long time, even when Bogo's voice lifted in shrill, authoritative rage.

Bogo finally opened the door and jumped out of the car and stood on the road beside Durell, who remained behind the wheel.

"I don't know what to do," Amr muttered.

"What's wrong? What are you trying to get at?" Durell asked.

"This girl . . . she thinks I can believe . . . Oh, you don't understand, Sam, how it is with my people."

"What are you sore about, anyway?"

"Perhaps she has too much English in her—from her mother, I suppose. She says she will cling to me, no matter what happens."

"Is that bad?"

The fox face grinned, marked even then with the shadow of future weakness and evil. "I have rejected her. When I choose my wives, it is I who will pick them. It is not for you to understand, Sam. It is a matter of my honor."

"She's pretty young to worry about it, anyway."

"Zoraya is old enough. In my country she is a mature woman, ready to bear children."

Durell, who had fumbled with girls in the Bayous before

coming north, and who had dated Westover girls in Connecticut, found it all somewhat incomprehensible.

"Wait here," Amr said. "I must think. I will walk. Wait."

It was a beautifully clear dawn. Durell remembered it distinctly—the way the light lifted like a curtain over the broad, calm reaches of the Chesapeake. There were the cries of gulls and the sudden rush of wild ducks in the reeds. There was a mist over the water that turned to pure gold. It was warmer here than in Connecticut. Durell lit a cigarette and settled behind the wheel, watching the prince walk in dejection, hands jammed into his pockets, until he was out of sight.

Then he became aware of the girl's tears.

It seemed to him that the sounds she made were like the thin cries of a wounded bird.

He twisted around on the seat and looked at her small, huddled figure in the brightening daylight.

"Take it easy," he said awkwardly. "Can you understand me?"

"I am sorry. Please do not tell Amr that I wept. Yes, I speak English. And French and Spanish."

"I see."

"You are a good friend to Amr." She made it a statement. "He told me about you. I am afraid we were not polite, speaking so you could not understand."

"Here. Use my handkerchief," he said.

She blew her nose like a child. "I am sorry. Forgive me. I am—what do you call it?—rejected. Jilted."

"There is plenty of time to settle things."

"No, he will persist. He will not believe me when I . . . Even if I could make him love me, later on, he will not have me."

"Why?"

"Because it is his way."

"Perhaps you should be happy about that."

"Oh, no! He will recognize me some day," the girl said. "I will be patient. Some day he will need me and call for me, and I will be ready and I will go to him."

"Are you in love with Amr?"

She was silent. Her eyes reflected the gold of the morning sunrise. He looked at her and saw the strange confusion in her of child and woman—half sobriety, half mischievousness. Her eyes were tawny, liquid. Her face, half-molded as yet, partly screened by dark, tumbled, bedewed hair, considered him soberly from under her scarf.

"You are a good friend. Did Amr tell you I am his wife?"

"No."

"It is true. We were married four years ago."

"But . . ."

"Yes, I was only eight. But such things are done in my country." She laughed, almost giggled. "I can remember Amr now, sitting on all those cushions on the barada, glass-eyed, half-drunk with qat. They gave it to him to chew. He was so funny then, I—" She paused, and the tawny eyes darkened. "But something happened. There was fighting, and before the sun set I was taken away by some men who were enemies of my father. They held me in the desert for three days. And Amr, ever since, will not believe I was not really touched by them. Do you see? His honor, he thinks, has been injured. He will not accept me as his bride. He will never forget it. But I will never stop trying to persuade him."

"Then you do love him," Durell said.

"You are a kind man," she said quietly. "You are Amr's best friend, he told me. Some day, perhaps, you will be kind to me, too."

"If I get the chance," he said.

"The time will come. I know it. I shall never forget you." She paused. "Amr loves me. He listens to me, even now. But he will not yield." Then she smiled. "I won't forget you, either, Sam Durell."

In the long years since that dawn, Durell remembered Prince Amr al-Maari and the child-woman, Zoraya. He finally taught Bogo how to play poker, but Bogo returned to Europe that summer and transferred to the Sorbonne in Paris; later, when Hitler's armies smashed across Europe, the little Arab fox vanished for the duration of the war.

Afterward, however, Durell occasionally saw the small, handsome face in newsreels and society pages, and each time the sharply defined features seemed less clear, slowly growing bloated with dissipation and self-indulgence. It was said that Prince Amr's income measured a hundred million a year. For a short time he ran his sultanate with enlightened care, only to return it back later to his grandfather, the Imam Yazid.

Bogo never married. During the postwar years he brought his tiny nation out of the darkness of feudalism, changing it from a harbor for pirates, slave-runners, camel traders, and shepherds to an oil-rich land that eagerly embraced every vice of the West and every warped ideology of the East.

There was a time when Zoraya's pursuit of her desert prince

made fine grist for the society columns and the social sycophants of Europe. But never had Zoraya's photograph appeared with Amr's. He continued to reject her. He refused to
see her. Yet he did not choose the easy path of Moslem divorce.

And Zoraya moved into obscurity, her face denied to news
photographers. For Durell she remained the child-woman of
twelve years on that misty-bright morning on the shore of the
Chesapeake Bay.

You can never go back, he thought.

Whatever Amr was today, the Yale undergraduate was gone.
And whatever Durell had become, as he drove his Fiat along
the fine Swiss highway toward Lausanne, he was a far distance from his bayou boyhood and his years in New Haven.
He had even come a long way from the relatively simple days
of service with G2 and the old OSS. He had been manipu-
lated, by time and circumstance. He had been at war too
long, he thought, fighting in this secret war of sudden death
in obscure parts of the world.

Like his opposite number here in Geneva, Major Kolia
Mikelnikov, Durell had become a professional, a specialist, a
finely honed weapon for defense, a deadly mechanism for assault. He would probably stay in the business, he thought,
until he ended, through a tiny, momentary error, like John
Blaney, in Jidrat.

Very dead.

Chapter Five

THE HOSPITAL OF ST. HOMERIUS was midway to Lausanne in a piny valley on the upper slopes of an Alpine ravine. Dusk had turned the surface of the lake to lavender. Up here, a cool wind blew and hinted of the ice of the glaciers on the summits much higher up.

The hospital was one of those small, private retreats dedicated to the peculiar afflictions of Europe's rich. The main building was a large log chalet. Smaller cabins were secluded in pine groves along bark paths.

Dr. Franz Gehman-DeWitte made no objection when Durell sent in his name via a prim, starched receptionist. There were rows of chaises on the chalet's balconies containing bundled, motionless forms, like mummies turned carefully to face the setting sun, as if in some religious ritual. Nobody conversed. A hushed, exhausted silence hovered over the place.

Dr. Gehman-DeWitte looked exhausted, too. A thin bearded man with the avaricious eyes of a racketeer rather than a doctor, he sat glumly behind his desk and smoked a cigarette in an elaborate filter holder. He stood up briefly as Durell was ushered into his office, and listened, again with an air of exhaustion, when Durell introduced himself and asked if it were possible for him to see the Prince of Jidrat.

"No, not possible," DeWitte said promptly. His English had a strange Bronx flavor. "Item one, Prince Amr saw no one, absolutely no one, while he was here. He refused all interviews, all contact with the other patients, refused to cooperate, refused to take medication, refused to act like a rational human being."

"You put it all in the past tense, Dr. DeWitte."

"Correct. He is gone. This morning. And good riddance."

"Doctor, I would like to be sure this is not just another measure used by the prince to avoid people while he . . . uh . . . is resting here. He *would* like to see me. I am an old friend."

"You don't look like one," the doctor said sourly.

"I beg your pardon?"

"You do not appear to be a man addicted to drugs, women, liquor, or any other dissipating vice known to men—although your prince, I admit, has invented several new depravities of his own."

Durell smiled. "You seem happy to be rid of him."

"I am. He is an animal."

"But with a fat wallet."

"I will never accept him here again. I do not care who knows it. I could not endure such ignominies, such tantrums, such grossness, such inhuman cruelties."

"Surely he can't be as bad as all that."

The doctor drew a deep breath. "I divulge no medical confidence when I tell you the prince came here in a delirium induced by drugs, exhaustion effected by over-indulgence in rather exotic sexual exercises, and an acute case of indigestion. God knows what he eats. The man is grossly overweight, flabby, neurotic, self-indulgent. His blood is poisoned, his liver is enlarged, his thyroid is totally abnormal. And you say you are his friend, M'sieu Durell?"

"I was. A long time ago."

"Then you would not recognize him today."

"Perhaps not. But I must see him."

"He is not here. Search if you wish. I do not care. He is gone, bag and baggage. The moment he was able to wobble away on his fat legs." Dr. Gehman-DeWitte drew a deep, shaky breath, yanked open his desk, pawed among papers, and tossed down a check drawn on a Swiss bank for a sum equivalent to twenty thousand American dollars, payable to the Hospital of St. Homerius. "Never again," the doctor whispered. "It is not enough. I will not tell you what indignities he inflicted upon me and my staff while he was here. But never again."

Durell said, "And he left this morning?"

"In his own car. A Mercedes. He drove it himself."

"Do you know where he went?"

Dr. Gehman-DeWitte flung out his arms. "To Cannes, of course. To his villa there."

Durell drove to the French Riviera that night, stopping at a small pensione near the French-Italian border for four hours of sleep. He was not followed. He was careful on the Alpine highways going south during the night, thinking of Major Kolia Mikelnikov's mission, but nothing happened. He slept with a gun at his hand in a rough farmhouse that took in European tourists. He rigged the heavy door so no one could touch it without waking him at once, and his window overlooked the dooryard, a sheer drop of over thirty feet. He slept lightly, but without interruption, ate breakfast with the Italian farmer and his wife, speaking to them in their dialect, and then drove on through the customs barrier into France.

At Cannes, he did not bother hunting for a place to sleep. He phoned Haggarty, then went down to the waterfront beyond the beaches and the expensive hotels. Cannes was full of Americans. The sun shone, the sea sparkled, the Gallic air was gay and festive. He drove to an inexpensive hotel near La Bourginon and asked for a man named Leonard Cato. He was advised by the clerk that Cato could be found, as always, at the Miramar. Durell telephoned, mentioned his name, accepted an invitation for a drink, and drove back to meet Leonard Cato at the Café de Paris.

Cato was an American expatriate whose column of Riviera gossip was eagerly read by the world of fashionable nobility and café society that haunted the beaches of the Mediterranean, as well as the clubs of Rome and Paris. Sometimes Cato's items were reprinted by Stateside news syndicates. He was a neat and elegant man, and all traces of his home town of Emporia, Kansas, were long since buried beneath his cultivated continental manner. He looked like a perfumed clerk from a Paris fashion salon, but his small eyes were sharp and intelligent and his handshake was remarkably firm as he greeted Durell.

He did not know Durell was in K Section. But Cato had often been tapped for past services, and he knew at once that more demands were about to be made of him. He was reasonably trustworthy and his information was dependable. Durell had met him several times on past assignments.

"My dear boy," Cato greeted him. "What brings you out of the swampy bayous of Louisiana Province to this decadent splendor?"

Durell ordered apéritifs and considered the crowds of oddly dressed tourists nearby. He saw nothing to concern him. Quietly, he told Cato what he wanted.

"Impossible, dear boy," Cato said promptly.

"I'm sure Amr will remember me," Durell said, "if I can reach him."

"Of course. If he were sober. Or not drugged. Or not wallowing under the imported female flesh he smothers himself with. But it is impossible." Len Cato smiled. "Why renew old acquaintance with this barbarian, Samuel? He is not your type, I assure you."

"It's a business matter, Cato. I'm acting as middleman."

"I see. And you have a generous expense account?"

"Five hundred for you, if you can get me to the prince."

"In dollars?"

"Yes."

Cato said musingly, "I could use the money, my Cajun friend. I will not press you about the principals for whom you act. I can guess. And you've come to the right man, of course. No one in all Europe can help you as I can, Samuel."

"I'm counting on that," Durell said patiently.

"The rumor goes that the prince's private oil preserves will not be in his name much longer, if the Q'adi and Colonel Ta'arife have their way. But I suppose that's a problem best left to the diplomats, eh?" Cato laughed. "Amr has millions cached away in Swiss banks, anyway. I wonder why it is that the good of this world are always poor and noble, and those who are evil seem endowed with luxury and perverted pleasures?"

"That cause-and-effect relationship could be reversed, Cato. Where is he? At his villa near Menton?"

"So they say. It's been a dull season, according to the Count d'Igli. Amr was here briefly. He went aboard the count's yacht. They sailed away and are due back this weekend. If I could work this into a few columns for the Sunday supplements back home this time—"

"No publicity," Durell said. "When can you get me to the prince?"

"This weekend. Four days. D'Igli invited me—"

"Too late," Durell interrupted. "I can't wait four days."

"My dear Samuel, he is at sea, aboard d'Igli's yacht."

"Where did they go?"

Cato sighed. "To Zoraya."

Durell was silent. In the slant of noon sunlight, hot and brilliant through the date palms on the avenue, he saw the passing crowd under the bright awnings, saw the terraces and pennons and animated faces of the passers-by. Leonard Cato suddenly seemed remote. Durell wondered which eyes among those in the passing crowd had found him out and marked him for ensnarement and death. He knew that Mikelnikov, under pressure of direct orders from Moscow, would not give up after the failure in Geneva. It must be important, Durell thought; he, himself, was important because of his potential influence on a dissolute Arabian prince from a tiny sultanate that could turn the world upside down if things went wrong there. Jidrat could erase this bright, gay scene in a rain of deadly ashes that would darken the earth forever. . . .

"Yes, he has sailed to see Zoraya," Cato said suddenly.

"In Elba?" Durell asked.

"Ah, you know of that?"

"I know that she has been living there, in seclusion."

"Zoraya, the fabulous and secret woman of mystery." Cato sighed. His eyes mocked his own words. "She can help you see Amr, if he visits her there—and if she cares to help. You know, they seem to have an agreement. If she insists on seeing him, he consents. It does not happen often. Their meetings, of course, always end in humiliation for her. You know the story, of course . . . married as children—"

"Yes, I know it," Durell said.

"Then go to Zoraya, in Elba. Perhaps you and I, with our Western orientation, will never understand their relationship. But it is as if their destinies are forever intertwined, and they both know this and accept it. They meet now and then, briefly, secretly. Of all the folk in Cannes who would give small fortunes to know where the prince has sailed on d'Igli's yacht, only I know the truth. You see, you get a bargain from me. I am truly a patriot, after all."

"For five hundred dollars," Durell said grimly.

"Payable now." Cato shrugged elegant shoulders. "As to Zoraya's influence on Amr, no one can understand these things. Why she should continue to languish for a sight of his bloated face . . ." Cato laughed again. "I tell you a secret, Samuel. Emotions bore me. Myself, I have none."

"Only greed."

"Ah. True. I sell rumors and speculations. I tell tales of secret meetings between star-crossed people, of a day spent on someone's yacht or on the terrace of an Elbani village. They walk together, hand in hand. They say she is remarkably beautiful. Remarkable. A serene and lovely woman patiently waiting, in medieval seclusion. It will make a classic love story, one day, when it is understood better."

"When did they meet last?" Durell asked.

"Over a year ago, when she retired to Elba. You can depend on it, Samuel—Amr has gone there. My information is always correct."

"All right, Cato." Durell took out his wallet and paid the slender, elegant little man from Emporia, Kansas. "Thanks a lot."

"Merci mille fois," Cato said. "Would you mind taking care of the check here, too?"

He drove to Piombino, on the Italian coast, via the Italian Riviera. It was a familiar drive, and he handled his small car expertly on the mountainous coastal roads. Nevertheless, the trip took most of the day and he was too late for the afternoon ferry that sailed between the mainland and the looming mountains of Elba, storied exile of the Emperor Napoleon, seven miles across the water from the coast.

He called Haggarty once more, using the private number in Geneva. "I'm going on alone. You won't hear from me until I get to Jidrat," he said.

"You seem to be taking the long way around, Cajun. But don't waste time. I've got a dispatch from Washington. The cork is ready to pop off the bottle. Revolution any minute. We need the prince there."

"I'll do what I can."

He found a small hotel on the outskirts of the small industrial town with its iron smelters, and ate quietly in the dining room, watching the other travelers who checked in. He saw no one familiar, nothing dangerous, yet his sixth sense nagged at him. He felt that he was being watched.

He slept that night with a chair against the door and his gun ready at hand. The air was heavy and breathless, smelling of the raw molten iron of Piombino's smelters. For some reason this made him recall the smell of the bayous in the heat of summer, and he thought of the shade of the towering gum and cypress trees, the quiet flicker of sunlight on the black water, the hum of insects, the drowsy heat, the sense that all life paused and breathed easily in the heat of the summer afternoon. He slept and dreamed of the bayous, and awoke in the morning with the gun gripped in his hand and sweat bathing his body.

A brassy sun shone on the Mediterranean. He paid to transport his Fiat to the island, and the morning ferry, which ran on a reasonable schedule, took him to the harbor of Portoferraio before noon, along with a cluster of tourists, a group of Swedes and Germans, a French hiking club, and Italian relatives of the Elbani from the mainland.

There was a mist over the water that the sun failed to dispel, but the harbor view was impressive with its glimpse of the towering fortifications built by Cosimo I de' Medici to repulse the Dragut of Tripoli in 1552. The battlements stood like dream illustrations from a child's fairy-tale book. Portoferraio's quayside was crowded when they landed, although most of the fishing boats were already out to sea. There was a delay until Durell retrieved his Fiat, and he singled out a tall, thin boy to watch the car while he walked off the quay through the tall Florentine gate cut into the ancient wall of the town. Directly beyond was the cosmopolitan Piazza Cavour, a broad cobblestone street with flagged walks and shops and outdoor cafés. Durell walked under brightly hued awnings and listened to the chatter in a dozen languages, glimpsed the market stalls of the Piazza della Repubblica, and turned back to the Bar Roma, where he ordered a cappucino.

The same fat Swiss who had followed him in Geneva in those moments before the truck smashed into his telephone booth suddenly appeared out of the passing crowd, walking quickly, wiping his red face with a large handkerchief.

Durell finished his cappucino and watched the fat man make a circuit of the Piazza Cavour without once looking his way.

It was not a coincidence, of course.

The fat man wore a dark suit and a high stiff collar and carried a furled umbrella. Durell considered the umbrella and did not like it. He wondered if the fat man was a deliberate lure to distract his attention, and he searched the other people around him carefully. He concluded that the fat man was alone. The Swiss by this time had gone into the Bar Roma and was talking to the headwaiter. Durell waited until the man came out again, and then it was his turn.

A twenty-dollar bill bought the information he wanted.

Inquiries had been made about the Princess Zoraya. Everyone knew, of course, that she lived in her villa on the Gold Coast, where Roman and exiled Russian nobility still held sway. Yes, the Prince of Jidrat had arrived this morning on the Count d'Igli's yacht. He was at the Count's villa, beyond the walled town of Marciana Alta. Did the signor know about the hermitage up there, and the Cassetta Napoleone and the Cassetta Walewska? A fine old story about the emperor and his romance during his stay in Elba. Of course, the Elbani embellished the tale each year, for tourists, but the truth of the matter. . .

Durell learned the way to Zoraya's villa and was advised against driving there without an experienced guide.

For a small fee . . . No, signor, there was no telephone. As for the Swiss gentleman—yes, he was inquiring about the Prince of Jidrat. Everyone does. One rolls the eyes, purses the mouth, looks shocked and delighted. It is said there is already a wild party in progress at d'Igli's villa. The women were brought over from the mainland, of course. Disgraceful, with the poor Princess Zoraya so near at hand. As if the prince deliberately sought to humiliate her. All of Elba discussed the affair. . .

Durell gave the man another twenty dollars and left.

The Swiss had disappeared.

Durell's car was parked on the sunlit quay, surrounded by passengers for the ferry which was already loading for its return trip to Piombino and the mainland. The tall boy guarded the Fiat ferociously. Durell thanked and paid him, checked directions to Marciana Alta, and drove off through the crowded streets of Portoferraio.

The day was hot. The mist had lifted off the sea, but high in the mountains of the island it clung like thick cotton. Once out of the main port, the Fiat struggled up and up, away from the harbor with its fantastically jutting battlements. Far across the channel, the mainland of Italy loomed through the mist, dimly seen, even as it had been during Napoleon's exile here. The roads were lined with masses of white lilies, wild roses, marguerites, and tiny orchids. There was little traffic. He was careful in passing a line of ox carts and peasants in Elbani costumes. A group of chattering, dark-skinned women fell silent and stared with curious eyes at the little car struggling up from the coastal level. Ahead were woodlands of pine and cypress, chestnut, and almond trees. The road made an abrupt curve around an arm of the mountain and the whole coast suddenly came into view, the length of the island seen as a tumbled, mountainous mass rising from the sea. Everywhere the land fell downward in rugged folds, with vineyards and pastel houses clinging to rocky cliffs. Ahead were the Gold Coast villas, in pinks and greens and creams and yellows, perched above their sandy private beaches.

It was at one of the switchbacks that Durell realized that the fat Swiss was following. He could look back and down the pine-grown slope to the road he had just covered, a hundred feet below. An open Mercedes touring car was coming up fast, raising a tumble of dust behind it. Two men were in it. The one driving was thin; he wore a seersucker suit and a battered Panama straw. Beside him, peering anxiously upward, was the small fat man.

Durell pushed the little Fiat harder, but the series of sharp switchbacks and impossible grades made the car labor and cough and lose momentum. He took his gun and put it on the seat beside him.

The road was wide enough for only a single car, and was guarded at only the most dangerous spots by stone retaining walls. At more than one place in the switchbacks, he could look down upon his pursuers. The Mercedes had closed the distance by half. The fat Swiss looked up, saw the Fiat above him. The sun gleamed on the green spectacles, the round red face, the intense, hunched shoulders.

Then, abruptly, they were in fog.

The mist lay in a high valley just before Marciana Alta. There was a row of huge boulders poised in front of the town gates, a relic of Middle Ages' defenses. But now a village priest in black cassock sat there reading, and old men and women were gossiping near the walls. The whitewashed houses looked unreal in the moving mist as Durell drove through. He could hear the beat of the Mercedes engine now, loud against the village walls. Then the fog was left behind, and the scene below yielded to the reaches of the Gulf of Procchio.

His instructions from the Bar Roma waiter were to take the first cutoff to the left after the village. He came upon it almost at once, swung the Fiat into an even narrower gravel road, and the grade promptly soared again, through darkening pine and chestnut groves, with only here and there a glimpse of the Gulf and the sea, far below.

But he could not out-run the Mercedes.

He knew he was close to the villa when he suddenly found a proper spot and braked the Fiat in a rolling tumble of dust. The road was wider here, big enough for the Mercedes to go by if the driver so chose. At one edge of the road there was a sharp drop of several hundred feet to a rugged little fiord where the sea made a steady, growling thunder that echoed up through the jagged pines.

The Mercedes careened around the last switchback at a fast pace. The driver and his fat passenger saw Durell's Fiat at the same moment. Durell jumped out of the car and placed the dubious shelter of the little motor between himself and his pursuers. His gun was in his hand, but not visible to the others. He knelt in the dust, as if to examine the right front wheel of the Fiat.

The Mercedes braked, kicked up gravel, rocked to a halt. The driver got out, slamming the door.

"Juliano, be careful!" the Swiss called in Italian.

"I know my business," the thin man growled. He walked toward Durell at a stiff-legged pace. "You there. You are in trouble?"

"Stay where you are," Durell called quietly.

The man spread his hands. "But we wish to help, signor."

"Then go back. I warn you."

The Swiss said, "Very well, Juliano. Do it quickly."

"Juliano, go back," Durell said. "This man has lied to you—"

"It is only a little pain, signor." The thin man grinned. "Just a little, to even the score for what you did to this gentleman. These things are understood here."

"I did nothing to your employer, Juliano."

"He says you have desperately wronged him. Only a little pain will even the score."

Durell's mouth went dry. Suddenly, the Elbani held a knife and it glittered in the white mist that drifted across the road. Far below, there was the crash of the sea below the pines that grew in the fiord. The thin man moved closer, on careful feet—like a dancer, smiling. His teeth were white and large and very even. He wore a large gold wedding ring on the hand that held the knife.

"Come here, signor," Juliano whispered. "It will be easier if you do not struggle."

Durell came around the Fiat with his gun in his hand. Juliano saw the gun and halted. He looked astonished. He looked back at the fat Swiss, but it was too late. There was the roar of the Mercedes motor, and the glint of dim sunlight on the fat man's green glasses. Then the Mercedes leaped forward at them—at the Fiat and Durell and the Elbani with the knife.

The thought flickered through Durell's mind that he should have anticipated this. The Swiss had used this method before. He liked to commit murder with moving vehicles.

The next moment he jumped for safety. His shoulder smashed into the Elbani and spun the man sideways. The knife jumped, slashed feebly at him. Then the heavy Mercedes was upon them, crashing into the little Fiat at the side of the road.

Durell fired three times at the fat face behind the windshield.

The glass starred and shattered.

The face dissolved in blood.

There was a thin screaming above the beat of the Mercedes' motor followed by the breaking sound of twisting trees as both Durell's Fiat and the Mercedes plunged off the road into the deep fiord.

Durell had no chance to watch. The Elbani scrambled to his feet, fell, and tried to get up. His face was twisted in agony. His leg was broken. He held out a hand in a wild plea for help, but it was too late. He lost his balance and went over the edge. It was as if a giant hand had suddenly plucked him out of existence.

For a few moments there was the sound of falling, of breaking branches, a distant crash upon rocks.

Then the rhythm of the sea was resumed in the fiord below.

Durell, who had dropped to his knees to fire at the Swiss, slowly got up. He walked to the edge of the road and looked down.

There was nothing to see. Both cars were gone.

Both men were gone, too.

He drew a deep breath of the air that smelled of the pines and the fog and the salty sea. His legs trembled for a moment. He looked up and down the twisting switchback road he had traveled. No one was in sight. Far up in the blue sky he saw the thin vapor trails of a squadron of jets on a training flight toward the coast of France.

He turned and walked in the same direction, up the hill, toward the villa of Zoraya.

Chapter Six

IN THE AMERICAN CONSULATE in Jidrat, T. P. Fenner stared
at the shattered office window and wiped his red face and
cursed the day he had let them flatter him into the notion
that he was a diplomat. It would have been all right if
they'd sent him to Paris or Rome or even Madrid, although
as a son of Oklahoma he didn't cotton to Spaniards who
might be related to Mexicans who, in turn, were a distinct
sub-species of the human race, in Teepee's catalogue. But
they'd sent him here—a hell of a reward for all the cash and
votes he'd contributed to the last political campaign.

He sat down angrily behind his desk, feeling a parched sensation in his throat, a prickly rash on his body. The air condi-
tioner was useless with the smashed window. And beyond the
broken glass was the wreckage of the garden, a degradation
inflicted on U.S. property by the savage, inflamed mob of
Jidratti. Beyond the broken window he could see the strange
five-story limestone houses of Jidrat, like the eyeless, bombed-
out cities of Europe after the war. In this case, however,
there was only the daily scourge of sun and sand, with a
wind like a breath out of hell, to effect this result.

He glared at the Arab who was trying to pull the rest of
the glass from the shattered window frame. "Impshi, ya
homar!" he rasped. "Get out, you donkey!"

The Arab turned at the irrational note in Fenner's voice.
Across the office, the aged Imam Yazid spoke quietly to the
laborer, who bowed and ran out. Fenner blew out a long
breath of air.

"Sorry. It's the heat, Highness. And the outrageous
insult to the American flag, the destruction of property—"

"The mob was out of control, Mr. Fenner. They acted
like animals crazed by the sun. I am here, personally," the
old man said, "to apologize and make restitution for the
damages."

Fenner felt as if he'd punched a sack of feathers. This
senile old man was interested only in his old books of
Koranic lore, but he could still roll with the punches. These

52

Arabs were smart and sly. They knew when to knuckle under. And they knew how to strike back—with a knife, in the dark. Oh, they were experts at that!

He thought of last night's riot with an inner shudder. Yazid's troops couldn't control the mob. Everything came apart: telephones and power failed and all law and order went up into the dark sky with the screams of the dirty crowd. The mob really ruled Jidrat, Fenner thought bitterly. Maybe Ta'arife was right. You needed a strong man, not this old geezer. What did Washington know about it, insisting the Imam be supported?

"I'll have to cable home," he said, aware of how the Imam had undercut his justifiable anger. "We can't accept this lawless threat to American lives and investments."

"Yes. I came to apologize." The old man looked tired. His hooded eyes in his old eagle's face were fixed on something in the blind mist of the past. "I ask again that Washington use its influence to bring back the prince."

"Impossible."

"To Americans, nothing is impossible."

"We have no influence with Amr al-Maari," Fenner said. "Anyway, he's not much, is he? No offense meant, but your grandson hasn't got the guts to come back here and face the music."

"He must be so persuaded, or you lose all. If Ta'arife and the Q'adi Ghezri win, as you saw last night, there will be nothing left here for your country, believe me."

"We can handle it all right," Fenner grumbled.

"But the world is complicated these days. When the English were here, at least they kept order. Today, a stone cast in Jidrat can smash the skyscrapers of New York City."

"Don't worry," Fenner said. "We'll take care of it."

"I trust that you do," the Imam said gravely.

Fenner stood up as the old man left. The Imam's guards, nattily turned out in khakis and snowy turbans, crowded the corridor outside the consulate. The old man walked feebly, as if exhausted.

To hell with it, Fenner thought. What was needed here was a platoon of U.S. Marines to put these people in their place.

He lit a cigar and went to the broken window. Beyond the tiled balcony was an open blast of afternoon sun. He looked at the wrecked garden, littered with filth and offal by last night's chanting mob, and then he stared beyond, to the shallow harbor with its tangle of crude oil pipelines intertwining like spaghetti to the concrete loading pier in the haze of the sea. Several tankers were pumping up the black liquid, like hungry beasts from some gargantuan, prehistoric world. The native dhows and trading vessels were tied up in the confusion of the waterfront. Nearer, the shrill ululations of food and coffee vendors, camel drovers and sheep herders, made a steady droning in the simmering air.

Fenner chewed his cigar and glared at the small tramp freighter that had limped into Jidrat the night before. She flew Liberian colors, but her skipper was American. And due here this afternoon, no doubt, with his tale of woe, expecting miracles from the American consul in this godforsaken hole.

Just for once, Fenner thought, let me go over to the bar at the Hotel al-Zaysir and talk shop with the oil men and hear the old Texas and Oklahoma drawl and drink some decent bourbon with men who made sense out of their lives. But he had the unhappy feeling that this wasn't going to be the day for it.

There was a knock on his door and he turned, half-expecting the old Imam back. But it was Esme Kenton. The Englishwoman, wife of the archeologist, Paul Kenton, wore a white suit, and her pale, sun-bleached hair was tied back with a simple ribbon. Her lips looked bloodless.

"Mr. Fenner, I want to know if you've heard anything," she began, in a tight blurt of words.

"Madam." He waved impatiently. "You see what happened last night. The police are busy with other matters."

"But you must find my husband!"

"I'm not responsible for British subjects, although I use my influence, of course. Colonel Ta'arife's police have promised to search the desert around Ain Gemilha for your husband."

"Ta'arife!" she cried. "But he killed your own man, John Blaney. Don't you know that? And now perhaps he's killed Paul!"

Fenner wondered who had ever described the English as an unemotional race. "Sit down, madam. You need a drink, now."

"I need my husband," Esme said thinly. "He tried to find out what happened to Blaney. That's why he's missing."

Fenner's stomach squirmed, remembering how Blaney had

looked, pegged out there in the desert with his body all carved up. "We know what happened to John Blaney," he muttered.

"But you don't know why," Esme insisted. "And Paul tried to find out. He went to the dig yesterday noon and he hasn't been seen since. The laborers at Ain Gemilha say he never got there. And they're all gone now, every one of them! As if they know Paul is dead and there won't be any more work for them."

"My dear madam, you're upset—"

"Oh, please," she said quietly. "Please help me."

Teepee Fenner shrugged helplessly. What did this plain Englishwoman in her thirties expect from him, anyway? It was up to Ta'arife's cops to hunt missing persons. And all that garbage about Kenton knowing something about Blaney's murder! She was just trying to get the weight of Uncle Sam behind her desperate hunt. No harm trying, Fenner thought, but he had other things to do besides upsetting the local applecart by insisting that the professor be turned up pronto. Probably the old boy had found some chips of pottery that had interested him and had just forgotten to come back. Probably nothing more serious than that, Fenner thought.

He looked at Esme Kenton with exasperation. "Your husband was warned not to interfere in political matters. What can I do now?"

"Won't you try to help?" she whispered again.

"There's a man coming here. He'll take charge of it."

"When? When will he be here?"

Fenner shrugged again. "I don't know. In a few days."

Esme Kenton stood up. She walked to the broken window and looked at the wreckage of the garden under the glare of the sun. Her voice was a tired whisper when she spoke.

"In a few days, Mr. Fenner, we may all be dead."

She walked through the crowded bazaars toward her house near the waterfront, heedless of the arrogant pushing of the throngs. A different temper ruled in Jidrat, as if the boiling sun had finally steeped men's brains in madness. She walked as though in a dream, thinking of Paul, and the fear in her was too great to be contained.

Her house faced the burning sea. There was a blank wall on the street side, facing the quay with its tangle of oil lines feeding the tankers. On the headland that formed the harbor there was no tree, not a speck of green, nothing but lizards and the sun and the muffled figures of Arab laborers. Yes, there were the limousines and the camels, she thought, the palaces and the hovels, and it was all insane, like handing a reckless child a dynamite cap and a hammer.

She had been all over the world with Paul. Their seven years of marriage had been a wonderful idyl, a dream of quiet joy and rewarding work. As an archeologist for a British foundation, Paul had worked in Yucatan and Malaya and now here, Jidrat, searching for the origins of the Nabatean culture that had spread over the Arabian peninsula into Sinai and the Negev, and merged with that of the ancient Judean tribes of Bible times. Ain Gemilha, the most promising site, was only six miles out of the city. She had been there twice today, but Paul wasn't there. And the Arab crews of diggers had scattered, frightened by something they would not tell her about.

Esme walked through her house into the walled garden in the rear, refreshing with its fountain and green oleanders. But there was no relief for her here. She called abruptly, "Tabib?"

He was there, the Sudanese Negro with three knife marks on each cheek. He was patient and strong. He had been with the Kentons since their arrival in Jidrat.

"Get the jeep, will you, Tabib?"

"Once more, Mrs. Kenton?"

She said tiredly, "We must keep looking for him."

It was only a short drive into the desert to the site of the archeological dig. The sun was still an hour above the horizon. The road spanned a wadi on a rickety Bailey bridge put up by the oil engineers and left as a courtesy to Paul. There was nothing to see but the high, flat mound of the ancient town buried under the debris of the two millenia since people flourished here in the time of Christ. Dear Christ, Esme thought, help me find him. Christ, help me.

Vultures soared in the burnished sky, far away. She told herself it was a dead camel or goat. Tabib stopped the jeep.

"There is no one here, Mrs. Kenton."

"Let's look again," she said.

There was the deep, uncovered well, dry now after a thousand years of disuse. Paul had laboriously uncovered the steps going down in spirals to the heart of the wadi floor. There were heaps of broken shards awaiting Paul's tally. Esme put a trembling hand to her lips. Carefully, she went down the steps of the ancient well, out of the blast of sunlight, and looked for any sign that might end her suspense and tell her about Paul.

Tabib went trudging over the flinty ground in the other direction, dutiful but stupid.

Esme paused at the bottom of the well. The sky seemed shut off above by the round opening over her head. A small heap of picks and shovels had been left against the wall of the cistern. If Paul had come here, there must surely be a sign—

She heard Tabib scream.

The sound was dim and faraway. Unreal. Like the scream of an animal in incredulous pain. It came and was gone, as if it had never been.

Esme turned and ran up the stone steps that circled out of the well. Her heart pounded. She came out into the blinding sunlight and could see nothing for a moment. The flat hill of Ain Gemilha looked as flinty and sterile as before. She could see no one.

"Tabib!" she called. "Was that you?"

Her words winged away into brazen emptiness.

Then she saw him.

He came running, arms flapping, with the staggering gait of a scarecrow. His white robe looked tangled and darkly stained. His mouth was open, and there was something strange about it. It was a dark, liquid orifice in a crazed face.

He made sounds of agony. He spit and coughed and choked on blood. The blood ran down his chin and he stared at her with unbelieving eyes from a dozen paces away.

His tongue had been cut out. He had been thrown to the ground, to judge by the dirt on his usually snowy robe. And his tongue was cut out.

"Tabib!" she cried.

He turned and ran away, staggering, and although she called after him and tried to overtake him, she could not. And presently he was lost in the orchid shadows of the desert and she found herself quite alone, her heart thudding enormously, as if to shake the world.

She turned and faced the empty, desolate digging site.

"Is anyone here?" she cried. "Where are you?" But her voice was swallowed by the grinning sun, and she cried again, "Come out where I can see you! Are you cowards? Are you beasts? Why did you do it?"

The desert offered no answer.

She sat down and wept in total agony of spirit.

When the sun went down and the chill night touched her, she knew that Tabib would not come back. He had been silenced forever. Whatever he had found was gone with him. So she walked slowly back to the jeep and drove across the Bailey bridge again, toward Jidrat.

Colonel Ta'arife also made appropriate apologies to T. P. Fenner. They sat in Bombay chairs on Fenner's balcony, behind the screen that hid them from the darkening street below. The colonel drank black coffee from a small brass cup. Fenner preferred bourbon. He had managed to kill most of a quart today.

"If there were a change in government," Ta'arife said blandly, "you could be assured that the restlessness would end. The people are disturbed by the rule of a senile old man. Imam Yazid has outlived his day, Mr. Fenner. Surely your government must understand that new ideas, new blood, youth—all this must be given an opportunity to rule." Ta'arife paused and smiled. "We would, of course, maintain the strictest neutrality."

"We?"

"I would be a part of the new government," Ta'arife said.

"That's settled, is it?"

"Yes. The Q'adi and I are agreed."

"That's the part I don't like," Fenner said bluntly. He spread his knees to ease his solid little paunch. "This Q'adi Ghezri, always going around in that black outfit, riding his white donkey—he looks like a lunatic to me. One of them radicals, like. A fanatic, y'know?"

"He will serve his purpose," Colonel Ta'arife said.

"Hum," Fenner said.

"If you could advise your government to be favorably disposed, to help us with money and arms, then perhaps . . ."

"Impossible. We won't interfere."

"Non-interference, too, if we could count on it, would help," Ta'arife murmured. He stood up, slender, elegant, a whip of a man with dark eyes that could hypnotize a crowd like the eyes of a snake holding a bird in its grip. "You understand that the mob violence last night was unavoidable? If matters threaten again, you will be warned, of course. And it will happen once more so long as Yazid rules here."

"Any further damage to U.S. property—"

"Will be paid for. I promise."

"I reckon that's all you can do, then," Fenner said grudgingly.

The colonel turned to go, then paused as if in afterthought. "One more thing, sir. The Liberian freighter that came into harbor this afternoon—the one with engine trouble?"

"Nothing to do with me," Fenner said promptly.

"The captain is American. He has asked permission to come ashore, urgently, to see you. We insist that his vessel be searched for contraband, you know."

"Contraband? The ship's engines broke down. He didn't choose to make port in Jidrat."

"We don't know that. We must always be alert."

"Against what? You're seeing ghosts, Colonel."

"Perhaps. But you do not object to our search of this ship?"

"Not my jurisdiction," Fenner grunted.

He drained the last of his bourbon as Colonel Ta'arife went out.

The captain of the *Atlantic Maid* was Thomas MacPherson. He was in his late fifties, gaunt and weather-beaten, with an ugly face and a massive chest and a habit of chewing, not smoking, cigars. He had been in the merchant marine since he was fourteen, and he knew the Arabian Sea and its dangers as he knew the craggy contours of his face. He carried a mixed cargo of raw rubber, spices, coffee, and hides from Indonesia and Malaya to the ports of Greece and the southern Mediterranean.

The *Atlantic Maid*, five thousand tons, was a rusty relic of thirty years at sea, with ancient engines and equipment. It was bad luck, however, that they'd had to put into Jidrat for repairs. MacPherson knew all about this cruel coast. He could smell political trouble in all the corners of the world, and he would have preferred to drift at sea while Kuhlman, his engineer officer, struggled to set things right down below. But parts were needed and there were Americans in Jidrat who could help. So there really hadn't been a choice.

But it was a tough shake for the girl.

Tom MacPherson always sailed with trouble, but it hadn't made him callous to the suffering of others. He firmly believed that the major trouble with the world came from the fact that most people failed to pause and listen to the pitiful cries for help that came from those less fortunate than themselves.

He certainly felt sorry for the girl.

She said her name was Naomi Haledi. She came aboard in Singapore, a brisk dark-haired woman, far too pretty to be traveling alone, he thought. But there was a business-like competence about her, an attitude that brooked no nonsense, when she asked for passage to Athens or Haifa via Capetown, as the *Atlantic Maid*'s itinerary advertised.

She was an Israeli, she said, the representative of a, potash and cement factory in Beersheba. She spoke English with an accent that told MacPherson she had been born in Europe, possibly Hungary. Her big, almond-shaped eyes had seen enough to match even MacPherson's book of troubles at sea.

There was room aboard for four passengers, but she was the only one booked for the trip. Miss Haledi came aboard with a briefcase full of contracts, a feeling of satisfaction at having made a successful trip, and enthusiasm over the prospect of a four-week rest while the *Atlantic Maid* slogged to Karachi and across the Indian Ocean to Capetown and then up along the old Gold Coast of Africa to the Mediterranean.

Now she was in trouble. The worst sort of trouble.

It was exactly the sort of thing she had tried to avoid.

MacPherson had asked her bluntly why she hadn't flown home, using a commercial airline instead of his bumbling, rusty teakettle of a boat. She said she wanted a vacation; the time was coming to her. All the data and contracts she had collected had been mailed home to Israel, except for unimportant documents. She had been ill, too. The doctor in Singapore had recommended the sea voyage.

MacPherson wondered if it was nerves, although she seemed calm enough when she booked passage. But he remembered now, as he went from the bridge to her cabin, that he had heard her weeping quietly, twice, during the hot, brutal trip around India.

He knocked gently and heard her speak, after a moment, in a voice both guarded and alarmed. "Who is it?"

"MacPherson, Miss. May I talk to you?"

"Are you alone?"

"Yes, Miss."

"Have the inspectors come aboard yet?"

"They're not due until tomorrow morning, I think."

The louvered door opened, and she stood there, squinting

into the huge westering sun that turned the sky into a shocking, incredible array of colors over Jidrat. She wore a white dress and carried her shoulder bag of brown leather. "Come in, please."

"Are you all right?" MacPherson's manner was fatherly. "You haven't stepped out on deck since we came into port, Miss Haledi."

"Best if I don't," she said tightly. "They will come aboard and my Israeli papers will make trouble for you. They may imprison me."

"Not while I'm captain of the *Atlantic Maid*."

"You could not stop them," she said gently. "They will call me a spy and seize your vessel if you resist. True, I could not know we would break down and come here for repairs. But they will not be so rational, Captain. You know this is true. You try to be kind, but what can you do? I can only say . . . I will not be taken from your ship."

"Of course not."

She shook her head. "You understand, I will fight them." She opened her purse and showed him a Luger. She held it easily. "I will use this first, before I let them put their hands on me."

"Now, Miss Haledi . . ." He paused, knowing that any attempt to ease the truth would only be met by her contempt. She knew the truth. She knew what might happen to her in this city of inflamed passions. He waved a big hand. "Put the gun away. It won't be enough, you know."

"I must try. That is all I can do."

"We'll think of something before they come here. Maybe I can dig up a British or American passport we can doctor for you. Anyway, I'll see the American consul again."

"Why should he help me?" she asked scornfully.

MacPherson had no reply. It was hot in the cabin. Moored by the quay, the old vessel absorbed all the heat exuded by the limestone hills of Jidrat. "We might smuggle you aboard one of the tankers," he finally suggested.

"They go through the Suez Canal. They would not risk their passage for me." She shook her head. "I appreciate your kindness in trying to help me, but do not trouble yourself more, Captain."

She closed the cabin door when MacPherson left and sank down on a bunk to light a cigarette. Her hands shook. Through the open porthole she smelled the brassy heat of the desert, the incredible odor of excrement and spices that came across the filthy harbor water.

All my life, she thought, I've been running and hiding. I thought I was safe when I came to Israel. I thought I'd come home. But there is no safety anywhere. One must live always in fear, it seems. Nothing has changed since Budapest.

She thought of Budapest, of her acting career, of her father and two brothers. All dead now, gone in that dreadful moment of fire in the square. She saw it happen. She saw Kolia give the command that killed them as he sat in his armored car, his face savage and unnatural.

It had been a childish dream, those months of marriage to Kolia before it happened. He could protect her and her family, she'd thought. But she hadn't married Kolia for that. She loved him—until that moment in the square.

Afterward, she'd fled through Vienna to Israel. She never went back to that little apartment she had made into a home for herself and her Russian husband. You began again and tried to forget. But sooner or later fate picks you up and laughs in your face and puts you down in a place of terror, like this. A place from which there can be no escape—except by death.

Chapter Seven

DURELL followed the maidservant, a demure, sloe-eyed Elbani, up the marble steps and across the balustraded terrace
that seemed to be pasted to the mountainside. The evening
was cool. The Mediterranean and the distant Italian mainland
were shrouded in pastel shadows. The wind carried with it
the sound of old church bells, the rumble of cart wheels on
the road below, the bellow of an ox, and the endless beat of
the sea.

The villa was small, and not pretentious like its neighbors.
He noted that the shutters were a faded blue and the outer
walls had once been a chrome yellow, but had been washed
by sun and rain for years until they were almost white. Wicker
furniture was grouped on the terrace, and Zoraya was there,
waiting for him.

He felt an unexpected anticipation. In his memory, she
existed as the big-eyed, frightened child in the dawn brilliance
of a Chesapeake morning, her head bowed against the Arabic
invectives delivered by a Yale student.

He did not know what he had expected, but from Cato's
words he knew she had become beautiful. He felt astonished
when he saw her rise and come toward him. For once, Cato
had understated the case.

She smiled, and extended her hand, and there was about
her the same air of anticipation as his, as if they were old,
old friends and not simply two people who had met long ago
on a misty morning far from this place. Each should have
long ago forgotten the other, but it was clear that she had
not forgotten Durell, any more than he had lost her image in
his memory.

"Sam," she said quietly. "Sam Durell."

"Hello, Zoraya."

"I always knew that you and I would meet again."

"You remember, then?"

"Of course. And you do, too. It is strange, is it not?" She
gestured. "Do sit down. I am happy to see you. How did you
find me?"

63

"For a woman with an international reputation for mystery, you were not difficult to find."

She laughed. "Mystery? I am a simple person, devoted to simple causes, Durell. May I get you a drink? We have some native white wine. A light supper? There is freshly netted fish, *pasterella* cheese—"

"Nothing, thank you."

"You look as if . . . Were you in an accident?"

"It was not an accident," Durell said. "My car went over the cliff, however."

She touched her lips in a swift gesture of dismay. She had grown tall. She wore a Hindu sari, a shimmering swirl of gold net around a body that obviously was full and mature and desirable. Her eyes were incredibly large—a clear and unusual gold—and he remembered the tawniness of her gaze. Under her wide, arched brows, her eyes expressed concern for him with an intimacy that was warm and at once responsive, as if, in their mutual memories of that Chesapeake dawn, they had somehow remained close to each other through all the years that had intervened. It was as if they were truly old friends.

Her complexion was English, inherited from her mother. There was strength and intelligence in her face. She came toward him and touched his cheek with wondering fingertips.

"I've thought of you so much. . . . It was not an accident?"

"No. Another car was involved."

"I do not understand."

"I came here to ask something of you, Zoraya, and there are some who would like to prevent that."

"Oh. Politics."

"You could call it that."

"I am not interested in politics."

"Are you interested in Amr?"

She said quietly, "I am still married to him. He could choose the Moslem way and divorce me, simply by announcing it three times. But he has not done so. I think he will never do so."

"Do you debase yourself with hope, then? You know what he is," Durell said. "Have you seen him since he arrived last night?"

"No."

"Will you see him?"

"If he sends for me." She smiled. "You think I crawl

to him. He has not forgiven the child I was for what happened the day of our marriage. The men who stole me are long dead. I can only keep telling him that nothing happened then, that I am still his bride."

"You can't still love him," Durell said.

"You know nothing of it."

"I'm sorry." He paused. "I meant to take it slower. I have much to say to you, Zoraya. Perhaps I have no right to say any of it. You are angry with me already, because of my clumsiness. I admit that I don't understand you or Amr or what is between you."

"You never will."

"May I go on? May I tell you why I am here?"

"You said your car was damaged, but that it was no accident."

"That's part of why I'm here," Durell said.

She stared at him with golden eyes, bright and enormous in the fading light of day. Somewhere in the chestnut trees behind the villa, a nightingale suddenly sang in full throat. The house was silent, as if listening. The wind was stronger. It pressed the girl's sari close to her slender body. Her dark hair moved with the pressure of the wind as if endowed with a life of its own, caressing her cheek, a tendril kissing her lips, curling about a small, delicate ear on which a large pearl glistened, opalescent and milky in the evening light.

"You are not the first to come to me about Prince Amr," she said finally. "To come with tales of danger and warnings of catastrophe."

"Did you believe the others?"

"No."

"Will you believe me?" he asked.

Her eyes searched his face. "I will listen."

"But you must believe," he insisted. "There will be no others after me. There will be no more time, after tonight."

"You come here out of the past with an urgency that is frightening, Durell. My memory of you is bright. You were kind that night, when I was so unhappy. I have thought of you often since then. I told you I would see you again. But not like this, not like this."

"I am sorry. We cannot control our destiny."

She said, "Do you think I am a fool? A silly woman devoted to a man whose acts of vice are an abhorrence?"

"I simply do not understand it," he said.

She said, "Then you are not here just as an old friend."

"Not entirely. But because of that, of course."

"They chose you because of that night long ago?"

"Yes."

"Your people have the confidence of arrogance."

"No. We only try to do our best."

"For whom? For yourselves, naturally. It does not matter who else may be hurt or what the results are to others."

"That's not so. They sent me, it is true, because I once knew you and the prince. But it seems I cannot reach Amr. He is well protected. So I am here. I came to you for help, for understanding. And perhaps, in doing this thing together with me, you will find what you have been searching for all these years, Zoraya."

"What thing is that?" she challenged him.

He looked at the villa. It was empty. He looked at the darkening sky, the shifting sea, the mountains up and down the misty shore. It all seemed empty. He knew it was not. He knew there was danger. He had the feeling that the Swiss in the car was not the only agent sent to Elba. There were others. There would be someone sent by Mikelnikov, and some others from Jidrat, to keep the prince here—stupefied by his pleasures—to see that he continued to wallow in his vicious pastimes and forget the reason he had been born into the world.

He began to talk softly to the quiet, lovely woman who listened. He told her what he could. Not all of it, but enough. He knew that much of what he said was known to her already. Her mind was quick and bright. She knew the tremulous balance of power in the world today. She knew that only a small pebble could tip the scales to disaster. A pebble in the desert sands of Jidrat, perhaps, hurled by wild-eyed Jidratti inflamed by impassioned promises of a new glory for Islam.

Finally he told her what he wanted to do with the prince.

She was silent, staring out over the terrace to the dark sea. He lit a cigarette, wondering where the Elbani maid had gone. He wondered if there were other servants in the house. He did not break the silence with more questions. He watched the girl.

It came to him that she was young and vulnerable, after all. She was a woman now, but her life was warped by seclusion. The fact that she remembered him spoke vividly of the rarity for her of such moments as that morning in Maryland. She remembered him with fondness, with a strange, immediate, compulsive affection that he returned without hesitation, wanting to help her, wanting to touch her and hold her and comfort her.

She said, "And if he refuses to go home?"

"He will lose everything."

"And if he agrees?"

"They will try to kill him. Perhaps tonight. What happened to me on the road here shows that they know I am here, and they know why, and they are afraid, lest I succeed."

"They?"

"Those who would take Jidrat into a world alien to Islam."

"But the Q'adi Ghezri is a holy man—"

"Crazed with a lust for power, for worldly immortality."

"And Colonel Ta'arife?"

"An imitator of dictators in Egypt and Iraq."

"Would it be so terrible, then, if Amr stayed here and forgot politics?"

"Should he forget his duty?"

"It is only a word, nothing more."

"Would he be a man here, or in Jidrat?" Durell asked. "You have waited so long, Zoraya. I think you love him. The reasons for love are beyond rationality. You want what is best for him. I say that death is better for him than to stay here."

Her lips were parted. "Yes," she whispered.

"And nothing will ever change for you. You will go on waiting, a mystery to the world, dying slowly each day because you know the things he does to destroy himself."

"Yes."

"Would you end it now? Tonight?"

She stood up. She clasped her hands and the sari rustled with a golden, metallic sound, shaping itself lovingly to her body. "I am not afraid. But I feel certain that I should not interfere."

"You should. It is your right. And also your duty."

"After all this time . . ."

"You can end it. Or make a beginning of it, for yourself."

She looked down at him. "Amr will die."

"We don't know that."

"I know it. It is written. He will die."

Durell was silent.

She said, "But I agree. We will end it. I will take you to him now."

"You need not go with me to d'Igli's villa. There will be people there and acts you should not see—"

"I know of them. I will go. I am ready now."

Chapter Eight

THE PLEASURE DOME of Xanadu, Durell thought, was never pictured as the Count d'Igli's villa on the island of Elba. Yet he was sure that never in Coleridge's opium-induced dreams were the pleasures he so vividly intimated as broad or as amoral as the evening affair in full swing when Durell arrived with Zoraya.

She still wore her golden sari. He had dusted the grit and brambles, token of his escape on the mountain road, from his clothing. He had not reported the affair to the local police. Time enough for that. Someone would find the wrecked cars in the fiord, and the two bodies also; but not at once, he hoped. Not until he had left Elba behind him.

The Villa d'Igli was secluded at the end of a guarded mountain road overlooking the Gulf of Procchio. The view was a wild tumble of mountains, and indented coast with the town of Portoferraio in the distance; nearer at hand were careful terraces and vineyards and winding rows of orchards. Far off over the water, the iron smelters of Piombino on the mainland cast a ruddy hell-fire into the night sky.

A high stone wall circled the mountain, a relic of an ancient Roman camp and a subsequent Medici fortress once built there. The wall was topped with broken glass and barbed wire during the war, when the Nazis occupied the island. The remains of a concrete pillbox imbedded into the mountainside had been remodeled into a gatekeeper's cottage.

The gatekeeper was a burly man carrying a sidearm. He looked at Zoraya and Durell and muttered, "Wait, please. You are not on the list."

The gatekeeper telephoned to the main house, out of sight behind tall pines. Eventually he came out and, with a sullen look, opened the gate without a further word, and Durell drove through.

There were at least a hundred guests, possibly more, Durell estimated, with a preponderance of women. There were not many young men. There were several famous faces that he recognized, loose and unguarded here, whose presence

69

would have caused shocked comment in some European
capitals. Music washed the cool night air with a persistent
beat. There were flood-lights that shifted now and then at
random, swinging over terraces, formal gardens of boxwood
and tall poplars forming *allées* that ended in dark coverts
where Roman antique statuary stood in marble nudity while
other movements went on beneath, below, and around the
shrubbery.

Around a huge swimming pool people ate and drank and
a swift, noiseless corps of servants worked diligently, dark
faces blind to what was happening around them.

There was enough to see; the shifting floodlights made
certain of that.

The bathers in the marble pool were all nude. It was like
a scene from an old Bacchanalia, Durell thought, a Roman
festival. There were fat men with dead-white skin and slim,
lithe girls obviously there for their pleasure, and several stout
women, with ugly waddling bodies, catered to by dark
youths whose adoring eyes and words created jelly-like
laughter in the mountains of flesh cavorting with them.

Durell glanced at Zoraya as they mounted the marble
stairs to the terrace entrance. She walked proudly, as if nothing existed to the right or left of her, as if unaware of the
sudden, stunned hush that followed their passage.

Two youths, both nude, chased each other toward the
pool, shrieking like women. In a corner of the marble stairs,
in temporary shadow, two women and a man were in a tangled, impossible embrace. Durell took Zoraya's arm and helped
her forward. Her lips were pale. Her large eyes stared ahead,
unseeing.

"Princess?"

Durell turned. A tall Arab in a snowy gown with a face
that looked as if it had been hacked with an axe out of
mahogany stood beside them. "Princess Zoraya . . ."

She looked up. "Hassan," she said.

"The prince acknowledges your arrival," the man said in
French. "He bids you welcome. He asks you to forgive him,
but you must wait."

She looked at Durell. He shook his head.

"We cannot wait," she said.

"Forgive me, sir," said the Arab, "an error was made at the
gate. You are not permitted here. You must go back, sir."

"No," Zoraya said. "Mr. Durell stays at my side."

"He cannot be permitted—the gatekeeper was careless—"

Durell said, "I am an old friend of the prince. It is important that I see him at once."

"At the moment he . . . he is not available."

"We understand," Zoraya said. "Nevertheless, you will take us to him now."

"Mr. Durell must be searched. If he is armed—"

"I am armed," Durell said.

"Then I must have your weapon."

Durell hesitated. A waiter hurried out of the French doors of the villa, carrying two buckets of iced champagne. Two maids trotted after him with trays of food. The villa reached in two long terraced wings, with tall windows facing the Gulf of Procchio far below. Music filled the air—a waltz now, but with an odd, suggestive rhythm. Durell looked at the Arab servant, Hassan. Hassan was built like a bull, with his ax-face and small black eyes. Durell hesitated, then handed the man his .38 snub-barreled revolver.

"Take care of it," Durell said. "I shall want it back."

"Hadr, effendi. You are from the police?"

"No."

"May I ask, then, why you come here armed?"

"I am always armed. As you are, Hassan."

The Arab smiled, this time with a trace of understanding. He bowed and said, "I cannot go to the prince with you, effendi. But he is upstairs, in the Pink Room."

"I know where it is," Zoraya said thinly.

She led the way. It was evident that she had visited the Villa d'Igli before, but not, Durell was sure, during one of these parties. Some of the rooms they passed were dark, others brilliantly lighted. The music followed them. There was a burst of laughter and applause, a woman's shriek of ecstasy from behind a closed door. There was the smell of perfume and food and marijuana. A very stout woman, naked from the waist up, stood at the foot of the stairs and blocked their way. Her eyes were pale blue, almost all white. Her pupils were tiny, vicious dots in the white blindness.

She spoke in Rumanian. "Oh, pretty. Pretty young girl. All in gold. And is your skin gold, prettiness? Let me see."

"Please, your Highness," Zoraya murmured.

"I shock you? These pendulousities disgust you, darling?"

"I must go up. Please."

"I want you. Get rid of this man," she said, not looking

at Durell. Her intense concentration on the girl was amazing. "Get rid of him at once."

Zoraya slapped her. The woman's jowly face shook with the force of the blow. The slap was hard, cold, deliberate. The fat woman sat down on the stairs and wept. Zoraya stepped around her as if she no longer existed and went up, with Durell at her side.

Motion pictures were being shown in a salon above. Tense and heated faces of men and women watched the improbable sex play on the screen. In another room the smell of opium was thick and cloying. Other music, thin and reedy, came from the end of the wide corridor. There was Louis XIV furniture and elegant tapestries and a high window at the end of the hall.

"This is the Pink Room," Zoraya said, halting before closed double doors. "It is reserved for the elite guests. Amr will be in here, but he will not be in the mood for interruption."

"We can't wait," Durell said. "But I'm sorry you had to come with me to this place."

She said, "I have seen and heard nothing. It does not exist."

Durell opened the double door and stepped in with her. Her golden net sari rustled faintly. She halted, stepped back, and he felt a quick tremor in her body. The touch of her body against his was like a sudden burst of searing heat.

No one troubled to notice their entrance. The avid faces were all turned toward the entertainer who moved into a spotlight at the far end of the salon.

There were perhaps two dozen spectators in the dim room, seated on cushions on the floor. Incense curled through the shadows. The music of a flute came from behind a series of screens blocking the windows.

There was a smell in the room that Durell could not at first identify. Strong, overpowering, musky, it made a primitive reflex prickle the hair on the nape of his neck. It was a smell of animal, of maleness, of deep and remote jungle.

Zoraya drew in a quick breath. Then the curtains at the far end of the room were pulled aside and the cat stalked onto the small, raised platform.

It was a black male leopard. It was *his* smell that pervaded the room, the essence of male cat that rippled through the mixed audience of men and women. A shuddering sigh came from someone in the shadows. The black leopard had a diamond collar that flashed and glittered against his ebony coat. The leash that held him was also jeweled, and at the end of the leash was the girl.

Her body looked milky against the jet, demoniacal blackness of the animal. She wore a thin robe and gold sandals, nothing more. Her breathing was slow and languorous, her eyes looked drugged. Her smile was distant, as if part of herself existed somewhere far away from this room.

The music quickened, and the girl began to dance around the taut animal, kissing its head and brow, running her hands down the strong back to the twitching tail that moved slowly, like a club, almost in time to the music.

An atmosphere of heat and breathlessness pervaded the room.

Durell searched for Prince Amr al-Maari. Zoraya touched his arm and whispered, "There."

He looked at her first. "Are you all right?"

"I . . . I think so."

"Perhaps you had better wait outside."

"No."

He saw Amr seated where Zoraya had indicated—in the center of the arc of rapt spectators on the cushioned floor. In the dim light, Durell was not sure that he hadn't been misled, after all. The man who watched the blonde dancer and the black leopard in their insinuating movements was far removed from the slim, fox-faced Arab boy of long ago. It was as if another image were superimposed, with the latest blotting out the original. Amr al-Maari had grown fat and soft, with a slack face and dull eyes, with a look of pampered pettiness around his full mouth. His body, under a dark crimson robe, looked pudgy. His black hair had thinned until his scalp shone through. He sat cross-legged and eager, captured by what unfolded on the stage.

Durell looked at the dancer and the black leopard again. The music of the flute was joined by the hypnotic beat of the native drums and tambours, a beat that slowly quickened and became more urgent as the girl teased the black beast. Once the leopard suddenly lifted its flat head and stared straight at Durell, green eyes blazing with a jungle fire more animate and brilliant than the sparkling jewels in its collar. Its fangs were bared. A low rumble came from its demon chest, as if it sensed Durell, the only man in the room standing, as an enemy. The heavy tail twitched.

The dancer, oblivious to danger, laughed and slid her body along the sleek muscular flanks of the animal. Her blonde hair fell to one side. Her transparent robe slid away and she was nude, writhing to the beat of drums that increased in tempo while the flute made its reedy, impassioned demands. The audience sucked in a collective breath as the animal swung to the soft white body and nuzzled the girl, lifting a massive paw.

For an instant the claws showed—gilded, sharp, unpadded. The male scent of the giant cat filled the room.

The girl cried out in taunting challenge, made a mewing sound, and stroked the cat, stroked it faster, stimulating the beast to a quick, twitching frenzy. She postured before it, writhing in an excess of impassioned frustration. Someone in the audience moaned. A woman laughed in quick, high nervous tension.

Durell looked at Zoraya. Her eyes were closed. Her face was calm, serene.

He looked at Prince Amr al-Maari. The man's eyes bulged with narcotic rapture. He called out something in Arabic that Durell did not catch and tossed a clinking purse to the stage. The blonde girl moved in overt invitation to the cat.

The drums beat. The tambour rang. The flute cried.

The leopard sprang upon the girl.

There was a long sigh from the audience . . . a stirring, an uneasy congestion of blood and passion. Everything in the room was dark except the unnatural spectacle of beast and woman. The leopard's claw raked a ribbon of red along the girl's white thigh. The blood shone bright. She seemed empty of pain; her head down, her form arched, her eyes blindly staring.

The curtains at the side of the room stirred. A man suddenly appeared, dressed in dark clothes, and another, beside him.

They both held machine pistols in their hands.

They looked at the girl and the leopard instinctively before turning to search out Prince Amr among the spectators.

Their momentary distraction gave Durell his only chance to counter the attack.

His shout of warning was like a sudden whipcrack that broke the hypnotic spell of music, drugs, and spectacle.

The nearest of the two intruders was a dozen paces away; the other, just a few steps beyond.

The first pistol chattered as Durell jumped. His outthrust arm knocked up the barrel and the stream of slugs smashed into the ceiling, cracking the crystal chandelier, stitching a row of black holes across the ornate murals, and then making the draperies across the room jump and quiver with a life of their own.

A woman screamed.

The leopard roared.

Confusion came, with a great surge, among the spectators, who scrambled in abrupt, stunned panic for safety.

The first assassin was unprepared for Durell. They had counted on the paralyzing effect of surprise. Durell followed his thrust at the gun with a quick grip on the man's wrist, a twist that brought a shriek from the man as small bones broke and the machine pistol clattered to the polished floor. Durell hit him once, saw the dark, Arab, fanatic face fall away. He glimpsed a balustrade and small terrace behind the draperies that had hidden the assassins, and then he turned to the second man.

The second man held his fire, seeking out Prince Amr for a certain target. He was short and squat, with a dark face, down-curved mouth, flaring nostrils, and glittering eyes that acknowledged his own peril.

The prince was rising, trying to get out of the crowd grouped around the platform where the girl and the leopard had been.

Then the lights went out.

For an instant there was a stunned hush. Then the cries and whimpers of panic came back, redoubled. There was a swift rush of stampeding feet. Glass shattered. A woman screamed in a high, thin ululation.

Durell, fighting hard to get to the second armed man, smelled the leopard.

Its hot breath touched his face. Its sleek flank brushed by him, a sinewy machine of murderous power. Enraged and inflamed by the interruption of its act with the dancer, it had sought out the source of the trouble with uncanny skill. It reached the second assassin before Durell. There was a thud, a shriek of pure, incredulous terror, and then a long, sighing scream of pain as claws and fangs struck deep.

Durell halted. He spun around in the darkness.

Zoraya spoke from behind him. "I am here."

"And the prince?"

"Against the wall. Across the room. That is where I saw him last. A coward. His face . . . his terror . . ."

"With reason," Durell said. "They ask for his life."

He carried the assassin's gun with him, holding the girl with his free arm. The leopard moved on, having committed its single kill, and bounded out toward the terrace, into the night. Then the lights went on and Durell saw the animal clearly.

It had paused over the second killer and stood facing the panicked crowd. Its tail twitched. Bloody fangs were bared. The Arab lay bleeding under its heavy forepaw, his throat ripped. The black beast looked ready to spring on the throng that pushed away from it.

Durell raised the machine pistol and squeezed the trigger. The burst of slugs ripped into the sleek body and knocked the animal off its feet. It got up, coughing, swinging toward Durell. He fired again. The echoing shots seemed to demolish the room. The animal screamed and clawed the air and fell over heavily on the body of the second Arab.

The smell of gunsmoke and the racketing, explosive bursts seemed to vibrate in the air. There was stunned silence again. Durell glanced at the stage. The dancer lay there, naked, staring sightlessly at the ceiling. He could not tell if she were alive or dead. He searched for Prince Amr.

"Over there," Zoraya said. Her voice was calm. Her pale amber eyes indicated the prince's figure. Amr was about to vanish through a curtained exit across the room.

"Come on," Durell snapped.

He ran with her around the perimeter of the salon. Now there was confusion everywhere; hysterics from the women, as well as from some of the men. Other guests from the swimming pool and terraces came pouring up the road stairway. Durell shouted, "Amr!" and then, "Bogo!" hoping that the old nickname would halt the running man. But Amr ran faster. Durell left Zoraya behind. Fear moved in him because he did not know how many others were in the gang assigned to kill the prince. He couldn't let it happen now. If he were quick enough he could turn the whole nightmare evening to his advantage.

He caught up with Prince Amr at the end of the corridor, yanked open a door, and thrust him violently through, out of the crowd.

"Who—I demand—"

"Shut up and listen," Durell said. They were in a bedroom with a high, canopied bed with the crest of the d'Iglis on the ornately carved cherrywood headboard. French doors stood open to another balcony above the swimming pool. The room was empty except for the bed. The door opened behind him and Zoraya stepped in. Amr's eyes swung in panic to her, and then widened.

"You! Why are you here?"

"Listen to your friend, Amr," she said. "Please, Amr."

"My friend? I don't know this man—"

"I'm Sam Durell," Durell said. "You remember me."

"Durell? The Cajun? But you . . . where do you come from, at a time like this?" Sudden terror dilated the Arab's flushed features. "You are one of the assassins? You led them here?"

"Don't be a fool," Zoraya said sharply. "I told you, he is a friend. Perhaps the only friend you have in the world now."

"No, no, it is too much, not a coincidence. You will kill me—" Amr's voice broke off in a thin scream. Turning, he tried to plunge through the open doors across the dimly lit bedroom. Durell caught him with two strides. His patience yielded to sudden irritation. He did not deny himself the pleasure of doing what had occurred to him from the moment he first arrived here.

He swung once, and his fist caught the fox face unprepared. The wild, dark eyes stared in stupefaction, and then glazed over.

Durell caught Prince Amr al-Maari before he fell.

Chapter Nine

DURELL hauled the unconscious man to his feet and slung him over his shoulder. He handed the machine pistol to Zoraya, who took it gingerly. Amr was heavy and limp. Durell stepped onto the terrace with his burden, looked down at the milling guests, listened to the confused hubbub. The guests were being collected by men in dark suits who must have been the private guards. Other men in dark suits came running from around the back of the villa. At the far end of the balcony Durell stepped into a dark, empty room, and paused. The girl was close behind him. Her breathing made a tight whisper beside him.

"Is there a back stairs, Zoraya?"

"Where do you wish to go?" she asked.

"Into the woods. Your house won't be safe. They may try for Amr again. The two men you saw weren't alone. If we don't get away quickly, we'll be trapped. Right now, I think the guards have left their posts on the other side of the villa. We've got to get away. We can't count on the police to help."

"You are right. And if you hadn't been here tonight . . . ."

"Perhaps I brought this with me, when I came to Elba."

"No, I understand Amr's importance," she said. "He has been approached by the Q'adi Ghezri and Colonel Ta'arife. Amr telephoned me last night; he wanted to know what to do. He trusted me, but—he could not resist his obscene pleasures." Her voice was bitter. "Come, follow me. I will show you a safe way out."

Her figure was a swaying sheath of gold in the dim back corridors of the villa. Durell felt Amr stir on his shoulder. He would have to talk fast and persuasively when Amr awoke. And there was no telling what drugs or liquor influenced the man now.

A back door led them into a small garden of boxwood hedges. Statuary gleamed dimly in the moonlight. The mountain air smelled of pine and the salt sea, a relief after the fleshy odors in the house.

"There is a gate here," Zoraya said. "One moment."

He had been right about the guards. None were in sight on this side of the villa. The panic among the guests had drawn away those who had been posted here. But they would be back soon.

Tomorrow, Durell thought grimly, there would be much to explain to the police. The Count d'Igli would probably relish the notoriety following the spate of wild stories and juicy morsels of scandal.

He followed Zoraya quickly down a short path between the hedges and abruptly found himself in untended woods beyond the landscaped grounds. The path pitched down sharply through groves of pine. The wind blew cold through the soughing branches, and shadows leaped all around them.

"The main road is just beyond," said the girl. "But we must climb a stone wall ahead. Is Amr very heavy?"

"He's not the lad he used to be," Durell smiled. "Is there any other way down the mountain except the auto road?"

"Only a few goat paths in the vineyards and orchards."

"We'll go that way. It's less dangerous."

They moved on in silence. The girl was hampered by her tight, golden sari. Moonlight guided them, sliding through the pines. Then the high stone wall surrounding the d'Igli estate loomed ahead. Durell paused, sweating under the weight of his inert burden.

"Can you climb the wall?" he asked the girl.

"If you look the other way. My sari . . ."

The man on Durell's shoulder began to giggle. Durell had only this brief warning that Amr was conscious before the man began struggling to get down on his feet.

"You both speak," Amr gasped, in English, "as if my life had some value. Why should you try to save it? My word, please put me down. This is most undignified, you know."

Durell let the short, fat man slide off his shoulders. Amr promptly collapsed to the pine needles on the ground. Durell propped him against the stone wall that blocked their way. "Speak softly, Bogo, or your throat will be cut. Do you understand what happened? The assassins in the house are not alone."

"I see only you and poor Zoraya."

"You will not see the others, next time. The next time they will not fail."

"Where did you come from, Cajun? I am still surprised—"

"I was sent here to help you."

"I heard that you worked for your government."

"Yes. They sent me."

"To save me? Or to kill me?"

"To take you home."

The man giggled. His mouth was loose. "Kill me here, then. Do it now. It will be easier and quicker, and all the same."

"No."

"I will not go home."

"I think I can persuade you," said Durell.

"I think not. Go away now. I command you to release me."

"You'll come with us," Durell said, "if I have to knock you out again and carry you some more. Take your choice. Walk or ride. But you come with us."

"To Zoraya's? She will kidnap me at last. She will take me to her nest after all her years of fruitless pursuit?" Prince Amr suddenly straightened, his round face now thick with anger. "Nonsense. It was Tarya, the dancer, I was to have tonight. A new sensation, you see. First the leopard, then the prince." He giggled again, his head lolling. "It is so difficult to conceive of something new for amusement."

"I've thought of something for you," Durell said grimly.

"Oh?"

"You're going to act like a man."

Zoraya got over the wall without help, and then whispered back that all was clear. Durell was not so sure. He thought he heard crackling in the brush behind them, the sound of swift, searching passage. He waited a moment, then ordered Amr over the wall.

"But it is not dignified," Amr objected.

"You will climb, or be carried over."

"Cajun, tell me the truth . . . where did you come from?"

"Out of your past," Durell said. "Now, climb!"

"If you strike an al-Maari, the penalty is death."

"Then I've already incurred that penalty, Bogo. Once, long ago, at MacTivers' place, remember? And tonight. Let's get over the wall. Zoraya is waiting."

"One moment." The prince paused. His dark eyes, searching Durell's face, reflected dim moonlight. His mouth opened slackly. "All at once I fear I am sick."

"You can be sick later. Are you less than a woman—unable to climb the wall?"

"I will climb. Under protest."

Durell had to help him. The man's muscles were soft. His breath came in short, uncertain gasps. There was a grunt as he fell to the other side, then Zoraya's quick, concerned whisper. Durell scaled the wall in one easy leap, then paused to survey the woodland behind them.

He had been right. There were searchers in the woods, swift and anxious, ranging through the shadows. He looked ahead, down the mountain slope. The road was empty in the moonlight. At least it looked empty. But he decided not to trust it.

It took fifteen minutes to reach the edge of the switchback. From behind and above the auto road came the sound of motor cars, and the sky was luminous with all the lights from the Villa d'Igli. The way down the mountainside had been rough, a stumbling flight through rugged brush and over uncertain hedges. Every now and then the prince slipped and fell and giggled, or cursed. Durell and Zoraya helped him up each time.

At the roadside he fell to his knees and stayed there.

"Get up," Durell said.

"I cannot."

"Do you want to die here?"

"I will die where Allah wills me to die."

"You would surrender like a weakling?" Durell asked harshly.

Zoraya murmured, "Don't. Please."

Amr lifted his round, soft face. He was covered with dirt, sweaty and shaken. His sleek appearance had been wiped out by their flight down the mountain.

"Where are we running? And why?"

"There is a plan to kill you, so you won't go home."

"Who wants to kill me? I do nothing but spend money and die a little, each day."

"We don't know who it is, for certain. Colonel Ta'arife, perhaps, afraid you will return to Jidrat and replace the Imam Yazid. You are dangerous there because you are still popular with the Jidratti. The people there are sure you will return to help them."

"Bah! The people!" Amr breathed in contempt. "Those filthy peasants. Desert kites. Eaters of camel dung."

"They're all yours," Durell said.

"Traitors. Capitalists. Reds. I do not care for all that confusion. I have my own interests."

"Drugs? Women?"

"Why not?"

"Perhaps because Allah had you born as a man; and not just an ordinary man, but an al-Maari, a Prince of Jidrat."

"I am not religious any longer."

"We'll see," Durell said. "Now get on your feet."

"But we are safe here. Go get a car," Amr said.

"We'll walk. And not on the highway. We—"

Durell heard the car coasting downgrade, just the rumble of tires on the gravel. It came downhill without lights, its motor shut off. But the red brake-light suddenly flared, betraying it as it came around the curve, shining through the flickering pines.

"Get down!"

They fell, side by side, to the pine needles beside the road. The car was a Lancia. Durell raised his head carefully and tried to see the men inside. There were three he was sure of. Two angular, anonymous faces in the front seat; another blurred shadow in the back.

All at once, before Durell could stop him, Prince Amr lurched upright. "It is the count!" he cried. "My friend d'Igli! He will help—"

"You fool!"

It was too late. The Lancia braked with a lurch and a voice called in Italian, softly, coaxingly. The prince was on his feet when the first shot came. Durell dove at him, brought him tumbling down, rolling across the highway. He did not have to give orders to Zoraya. There were more shots, quick and spiteful bullets that whipped overhead as they fell down the grade on the opposite side of the road. Amr had paused for one moment of incredulous dismay over the fact that his friend, the Count d'Igli, had betrayed him—and then instinct spurred him to try to save himself.

Car doors slammed, thudded, were silent. They were in a fruit orchard on a broad terrace on the mountainside, with the symmetrically shaped trees making geometric patterns and aisles in the moonlight. Amr floundered, fell, picked himself up again.

"Stop!" a man shouted from behind them.

Durell still had the machine pistol. He called to Amr and Zoraya to keep going, then turned to face the ridge of the highway above. Dark shadows moved, leaping down toward the orchard. He squeezed the trigger lightly and sent a quick burst of racketing fire over their heads. The shadows dropped away instantly. Turning, Durell ran again.

Two shots followed. They were not going to give up easily.

The orchard ended in a low wall that dropped to the next terraced field below. This new field was a vineyard. The sound of the sea came louder, from surf bursting against the rocks of a small cove below. A path led through the vineyard, toward the loom of a stone farmhouse. The house was in total darkness. From behind them came no sounds. The pursuit was momentarily halted.

The girl stumbled, and Durell helped her up. She leaned against him, breathing in tortured gasps. "I don't know if I can go on. My feet . . ." She had lost her sandals and been running barefooted.

Durell looked at Amr. The prince sat on the ground, his head between his knees. No help there, Durell thought. He looked back desperately. The sound of a motor suddenly came down the mountainside. Perhaps the pursuers thought it would be easier to follow by using their car. Easier, and safer.

"Where can we go?" Zoraya asked. "My house is not a good place."

"No."

"There is a beach nearby. It is supposed to have been one of the favorite spots of Napoleon and the Countess Walewska. It is secluded, although during the day the tourists come there."

"Can you walk there?"

She looked at the farmhouse. "Or perhaps in that barn . . ."

"It would be searched. The beach is safer."

"I can do it," she decided.

They went on.

A dog barked briefly at them as they passed the farm, but he was tied up, and there was no danger. Yet the shrill yapping gave away their position, Durell thought. He hurried the girl and Amr on. She knew the way. A series of further terraces, fields, orchards and vineyards, then another farmhouse, a darkened villa, and then they had to cross the road again. This time they waited until there was no chance of being seen—and even then they ran in the shadows, the prince staggering, breathing harshly, mouth open.

A small stone house stood on the beach in the cove under a grove of pines. It was dark except for the glow of the moon on the sea. The surf made a gentle splashing on the coarse black sand. Durell paused and let the girl and Amr sink down to rest. He was sweating lightly. He looked at his watch. It was only a little after ten o'clock. There was no way to get off the island of Elba now. And the only way tomorrow would be by the ferry to Piombino, on the mainland.

Zoraya said, "May I have a cigarette? Is it safe?"

"I think so." He shook one free of his pack and lit it for her. In the tiny bomb-flare of the match he saw that her face was not as composed as it had been before. It was as if, now that they had stopped running for the moment, everything she had tried to ignore by her strength of body and mind came back to overpower her. He felt a quick, deep compassion for her and respect for what she had that had carried her this far.

"What is it?" she asked. "Why do you look at me like that?"

"I was thinking of you when you were a child and we first met, that dawn, so long ago."

"I was not a child then," she said.

"You were only twelve."

"But I was not a child," she repeated. "And I remembered you, too. For a time, you made me forget my duty and my purpose in life."

"I don't understand."

"I was born to be the wife of Prince Amr al-Maari of Jidrat. To raise sons and heirs for his throne. It is an ancient, proud family. Its roots go back to the time of the Prophet. I was taught that my mind and my body were dedicated to perpetuating that lineage. Prince Amr is the last true male of the al-Maaris. So I am dedicated to him."

"That's rather a feudal way of looking at things, today."

"Yes. But my country is a feudal land, whatever modernism has come to it through the discovery of oil. Oil has not blurred or filmed my vision, Durell. I know why I am on this earth."

"You said you once forgot your duty."

She smiled. Her amber eyes were wistful and amused.

"Yes. You see, I fell in love with you, Durell."

"And you say you were not a child then?" he smiled.

"No, I was a woman. As much a woman as I am today. It was long ago, but I did not forget you, did I? I knew you at once."

He said nothing, and she smiled and laughed at something in her memory and smoked her cigarette. She sat on the dark, cool sand and hugged her knees. The golden sari was torn in places, but she could make rags look like the gown of a queen,

Durell thought. The moonlight tangled in her dark hair and shone in her eyes.

"I wonder if it was a mistake to see you again." she said at last. "I asked no questions. I believed you at once. I trusted you and went to d'Igli's villa and I saw things I swore I would never be degraded by seeing."

"Forget that," he said roughly.

"I cannot. I saw Amr. I look at him now." She turned her head and stared at the prince. He was sprawled face down, in the sand in oblivious exhaustion. If he heard their words, he gave no sign of it. The girl's voice hardened. "I look at you and then I see him and I remember how I felt about you, so long ago. And that is the mistake, I think."

"Zoraya . . ."

"Because I could love you again," she said softly.

Chapter Ten

THE STONE COTTAGE on the beach was vacant and they slept there, on the flagged floor. Durell watched from the doorway, the gun ready at hand. They might be trailed here, he thought. The enemy was always efficient, always dangerous. There was little time for rest, and no time to think of what the girl had said, or what it could mean, or if this complication could be turned to good or bad in the job he had to do.

The prince could be handled, at least for the next twenty-four hours, while the drugs and the shock of the near-successful attempt on his life made him pliable. Afterward, a lifetime of arrogant command and a habit of petulant demands and self-indulgence would make him more difficult. But by then, Durell decided, they would be safely on their way.

He sat in the dark and watched the silver fade from the surface of the sea as the moon went down behind the mountains of Elba. The thought touched him that Napoleon, a century and a half ago, might have sat here, too, looking at the same sea and the same land, and that nothing here had changed since then. He wondered what the Emperor had thought in his days of imprisonment here, seeing the Italian shore so near and knowing that just beyond were the shattered ruins of empire and glory. True, here he had hatched his scheme for the Hundred Days that ended in Waterloo and a safer exile on St. Helena. Napoleon had been fat and testy then, a victim of delusive grandeurs, the secret butt of many jokes told against him by the peasant Elbani who had seen conquerors come and go through the times of the Etruscans and the Romans, the Medicis and the Nazis.

The world hadn't changed much since Napoleon's time, Durell thought. Men still tried to shake the world during their brief stay on earth. They still brought death and misery to the millions who stood in their way. Yet the sea went on, the tides rose and fell, the moon shone, as always, on the eternal mountains and plains of the earth.

But today, eternity held a different meaning. Today the mountains and the seas were not eternal. Man had put his hands on the ultimate weapons of destruction. He could erase the universe, if he so chose—or if another Napoleon arose to try his hand at conquest.

Durell watched the shadows on the beach, the dark angle of the mountain path by which they had come down. Nothing stirred. There was no alarm.

There did not have to be, he thought grimly. Elba was a tight island, rugged and mountainous, but highly organized. They could not hide here forever. And there was only the ferry by which to escape.

They would watch the ferry, of course.

"Durell?"

He turned and saw Amr standing in the cottage doorway.

"I will talk to you now," the Arab said.

"Come and sit down, then."

"Thank you. First, the truth. Did you come to save my life?"

"Yes."

"For the purpose of using me later?"

"Yes."

"And so perhaps I will be killed in the end, anyway, to accomplish what you came here to make me do?"

"Perhaps. But I hope it will not end that way."

"Yes. Hope." Amr exhaled softly. "Well, you are still an honest man, Cajun. But I never learned to play poker as well as you. And I never could read what went on in that brain of yours. We were friends once, and yet we were strangers. We are too different ever to know each other as I would like to know you."

"Sit down," Durell said again.

Amr sat on the sand beside him. He groaned a little and said, "I must tell you, I am wounded."

"How?"

"It is a bullet, I think. In my side. I did not know it, at first. There was so little pain. And then—here—I began to bleed. The bullet went through my side. Amusing, is it not? I have heard of men being shot and not realizing it. It . . . I feel ill, now. I thought you should know . . . I need a doctor. . . ."

Durell had moved with Amr's first words and was kneeling beside him to gently tear away the moist, blood-soaked silk shirting. Amr made a petulant sound of pain. "Be careful, please!"

"Does it hurt now?"

"Naturally. I must insist on a doctor."

Durell said, "You were just grazed. It's a flesh wound."

"But it is my flesh, and I suffer from it, and I wish to have a doctor, please."

"You understand what will happen to you if the assassins find you again?"

"I am in pain! Are you inhuman? I command you—"

"Shut up, Bogo," Durell said. "Maybe some day you can punish me for insubordination. But right now I'm in command. There's more than just your skin to consider. There's Zoraya, for one—"

"I am not interested in a woman just now. I order you—"

"Shut up," Durell said again. "I'll bandage this. The bleeding has stopped. The bullet went in and out through soft tissue. With care, you could heal in a week. Meanwhile, I admit it is painful. And you'll be stiff and uncomfortable tomorrow. But that's better than being very dead."

"Am I supposed to thank you?"

"I didn't save you for thanks. I want to take you back to Jidrat with me. I want you to acknowledge your responsibilities and stop Colonel Ta'arife and the Q'adi from their inflammatory tactics, from turning the Moslem world upside down."

"Upside down from whose point of view?" Amr asked softly. His words made Durell glance up at him. Whatever dissipation the man had suffered, whatever damage was done to his body, the corrosion had not yet destroyed the keen fox-like mind. Durell grinned, and Amr said, "You think to set me on my throne as a puppet of the West?"

"No. Knowing you, no."

"I give you no guarantee, promise no favors."

"A fair deal, that's all we ask."

"And if I conspired with your enemies on the other side?"

"We know you, and we are willing to take that risk."

"You would gamble on someone like me? An evil man, they say, a lecher, a weakling, a playboy?"

"No man is altogether evil."

"I am," Amr said. "I admit it. I have made a career of being evil." He laughed bitterly. "To be a true Moslem, one must live up to the meaning of the word. Do you know it? A Moslem, in Arabic, is one who submits—to the will of God, of course. I have submitted to nothing and to no man. Do you know the five duties of a man in Islam? One must pray five times daily; give alms generously; keep the fast of Ramadan; make the pilgrimage to Mecca, the hajj; and last, one time in his life the believer must say with full understanding and absolute acceptance, 'There is no God but God, and Mohammed is his Prophet.' I have done all these things but the last. Though I have spoken the words, I neither understood nor accepted them. Once, when Zoraya was taken from me and my honor destroyed and I knew I had lost her as my true bride, I fell on my knees in the desert and wept and tried to feel the understanding of those words, to accept them, to submit to Allah's will blindly. I stayed in the desert for a day and a night and a day again, saying those words over and over again until my eyes were blinded by the sun and my tongue swollen by thirst." The man's words faded for a moment, and he sighed. "I could not accept. I could not believe."

"Perhaps such a day will come for you, Bogo," Durell said, after a time. He finished making a rough, but serviceable, bandage; a pad and strips that went around the man's fat, flabby chest. "This will serve you. I'll get some penicillin for you tomorrow to make sure there's no infection. Zoraya will nurse you on the way."

"I don't want Zoraya to nurse me."

"Why not? I'm sure she's competent."

"I heard what she said to you. You both thought I had fainted with exhaustion—which is what I should have done if it had not been for the pain of my wound. I heard her confession to you."

"It meant nothing."

"You think so?"

Durell paused. "Why won't you have her, Bogo? Or if you don't want her, why not divorce her and set her free?"

"The whole world asks that question. It is simple. I have answered it, but no one believes me. I love my pleasures, and I am not sure I want sons of my seed, heirs to carry on. You see, I know what I am. I enjoy being what I am. Do you think you can change me, Cajun?"

"I am going to try."

"Because it is your job? Because it is your duty?"

"Perhaps. And perhaps for one other small reason."

"What is that?"

"We once were friends," Durell said.

Amr al-Maari was silent. Like Durell, he stared at the dark sea. It was almost midnight. In the stone cottage, the girl slept. Durell had talked earnestly for an hour, but he did not know if his words had made any impression. He felt as if his voice had washed against a sponge and been absorbed without meaning; as if this man in whom he was supposed to inspire courage and political responsibility was nothing, a soft animal able only to recognize its perverted appetites.

He received no answer. No promise to cooperate. No agreement to return to Jidrat and take over the throne from the old Imam Yazid.

He felt as if he had expended all his energy and argument on a cipher. While he had talked, the prince had petulantly examined his wound, complained about the tightness of the bandage, wished for a drink, discussed the anatomical merits of the blonde who had danced with the black leopard, and chuckled over the eventual panic among the guests. The thin fox face that Durell remembered was soft and round and sagging. The eyes that once were proud were now either vague or cunning.

Durell waited. He had said all he could, tried to be as persuasive as possible. He did not know if Amr had even listened.

He remembered a night in the bayous when he had been hunting with Amodeo Talliaferro, from Bayou Peche Rouge, and Talliaferro had broken his leg and Durell had had to persuade him to struggle home through the swamps, with the whine of mosquitoes driving them insane, with all the dangers and terrors of the dark, dripping delta around them. They'd been only boys then. Durell had talked and talked, afraid to stop because he needed the sound of his own voice, and Talliaferro had needed his words, too, in order not to give up. They might have drowned, or been lost in the grim cypress bogs, or gone into quicksand under the gum trees.

He tried to remember what he had said to Amodeo. Anything and everything. About the mysteries of women, of the wide world, of people they knew in Bayou Peche Rouge. About his grandfather Jonathan and the old days on the Mississippi when Jonathan was a boy, when the river was wide and primitive and lusty, when the side-wheeler steamboats were an everyday sight, not just a rotting hulk in the mud serving as a home for Sam Durell and his old grandfather. Eventually, while he'd talked to Talliaferro, they had come to an old Indian chèniere and they followed the ridge of the dike to a road, and from there they had come to safety. All the time, Talliaferro had leaned on him, trying to spare his broken leg while they dragged themselves on, and afterward Durell realized that his friend had leaned on the sound of his voice, going on and on, as well as upon the strength of his body.

But he had run out of words with Bogo. There was nothing more he could say. Then, when he was silent, Amr al-Maari spoke.

"It is too much for me to accept. It is too sudden."

"Take your time. We have until daylight, perhaps."

"They will kill me to prevent my going home?"

"You have the bullet wound to tell you that."

"And you can get me to Jidrat?"

"Yes."

"And then?"

"Then it will be up to you."

Amr grinned slyly. "In Jidrat I could enjoy my revenge, Durell."

"Revenge?"

"I could have you shot for insulting me as you have done. Do you think I might order such a thing?"

"I don't know," Durell said. "You might."

"Yes, I might. It depends. But you can save me now?"

"If you want me to."

"One wants to live a little longer, naturally."

"Then you will have to do everything I tell you to do."

"Until Jidrat?"

"Until then."

Amr was silent again. The sound of the wind had left the pine trees. The night seemed warmer. The lights of an air liner, probably the Rome-Paris flight, passed high overhead. It seemed remote and unattainable, that world up there.

"I am weak, Durell. I have indulged myself. My enemies have been satisfied that I am not dangerous to them, if I continue this life. If I refuse to go with you, if I leave you now, I will be safe. They will know I have rejected you, that I will not play your game."

"Yes, if they believe you."

"Why wouldn't they?"

"They may not wait to ask questions. They didn't wait tonight. They bought your friend, the Count d'Igli. His villa was a death trap for you."

"Because they knew you were coming there!" the prince objected. "Only because of that."

"True. Otherwise, they laugh at you. They encourage your vices and look for the end of the al-Maari family. As you have been, you are dangerous to no one but yourself. I have told you all this," Durell said, "and now I am finished."

Amr said, "But I am a coward, Durell."

"We all know fear, at times."

"If I go with you, it will be only under protest. And I do not promise what I shall demand as revenge when we reach home. You are too strong. I resent this. I shall see what I can do when we are home. I want to see if you will weep and cry out for mercy. You trapped me, by coming here, and now I have no choice. They would have left me alone, otherwise. So you are my enemy, too, as well as they. Is this understood between us?"

"Yes. We are enemies. And friends."

"Later, I will not help you," Amr said. "I am ready to die here, if it must be. If it all proves to be too boring."

"You will not die," Durell said. "I will die first."

"For me?" The prince laughed.

"It is my job."

"How you must despise me now!"

"Yes," Durell said. "I do."

Before dawn, Zoraya awoke and led them down the beach to the cottage of a fisherman whose wife worked as a housemaid in her villa. The fisherman owned a small seine boat. For a sum of money that Durell paid out of the expense cash Haggarty had given him in Geneva, the fisherman went into Portoferraio and sailed his boat up the shore and brought it to the beach, where they waited. He reported much excitement in the town because of the events at the Count d'Igli's villa. Durell paid him an equal sum to forget what he had heard, and they sailed, not for the fishing grounds, but, for most of the day, southward along the coast, toward Ostia, the port of Rome.

The radio reported the mystery "tragedy" at the Count d'Igli's and the disappearance of Prince Amr al-Maari, heir to the throne of Jidrat.

In Ostia, Zoraya bought new clothes for herself and Durell walked through the Coney Island atmosphere of the resort with Amr and ordered supper for them, and then they took the crowded, high-speed suburban train, packed with chattering, sweating Romans returning from a day's holiday at the beach, to Rome.

In Rome, Durell telephoned Haggarty again. He picked up visas from a man in the lobby of the Excelsior Hotel, together with new airline tickets. Before the moon rose again, they were flying east to Athens, Ankara, and Karachi.

As far as he knew, they were neither followed nor suspected.

Chapter Eleven

AT DAWN, Naomi Haledi, the passenger aboard the *Atlantic Maid*, still had not slept. Now, as the brassy sun lifted out of the sea beyond Jidrat, she heard the city wake and stir, like a giant grumbling at being disturbed.

The sounds of confusion began with a flat, heavy explosion in the oil field. The concussion rolled across the harbor like the clap of an ogre's hands, and Naomi got up slowly from her bunk to stare through the porthole. In her confusion, she thought for a moment that she was back in Budapest, when the Soviet tanks returned to crush the rebellion. An image came before her of machine guns ravening the crowds her father and brother had joined—and then the image was gone. A sheet of flame leaped in fury from the oil tanks and lit the pre-dawn sky. Minor blasts followed as individual storage tanks went up. In the unreal light, Naomi saw the tankers at the end of the feeder lines coming alive, unhooking the loading pipes and getting ready to cast off their moorings.

It was stifling in the cabin and the brass rim of the porthole was hot to the touch because the old freighter could not shed the heat of the day. Naomi did not dare unlock the cabin door. Once, during the night, she'd heard the voices of an official boarding party, heard the guttural Arabic of a port officer demanding the crew's papers. MacPherson had protested in vain. Naked feet had slapped the steel decks nearby and bulkhead doors had slammed endlessly.

She had stood up, her heart pounding in familiar terror, her hand at her throat. She'd felt suffocated. Footsteps had come down the ladder from the captain's quarters, and another voice—one she'd recognized as being accustomed to cold authority—had called her name in English.

"Miss Haledi?"

She had stood in the darkness of her cabin—silent, not daring to reply. MacPherson's voice had rumbled in answer.

"Let my passenger alone. Her papers are in order."

"I must inspect them, sir."

"The girl is ill. I don't want her disturbed."

94

"I see. . . . Perhaps you can tell me her nationality?"

MacPherson had spoken without hesitation. "British. She's a lady representative for a Sheffield firm doing business in Singapore and Malaya. She took my ship for a sea voyage, for her health."

"You seem remarkably concerned for the young woman, sir."

"I'm only trying to be decent, Colonel Ta'arife."

"Decency is a virtue one cannot always afford. It is rumored that saboteurs are entering Jidrat. Enemy spies, elements subversive to the state. We must take precautions, you understand. The mob cannot always be controlled."

"Only when it suits your convenience," MacPherson had replied caustically.

The conversation at her stateroom door might have been planned for her benefit, Naomi thought. She sat down on the bunk, shuddering. Why was she such a coward? So many millions of her people had died bravely in Europe. Why couldn't she be strong enough to fight back? She had hoped to find the strength in Israel, in a new start, forgetting Kolia when she'd thrown her wedding ring into the Aegean Sea. But he had stayed with her, a cruel enigma, a distortion of love.

And she had never acted in violence in all her life. When her father and brothers had died under the guns fired because of Kolia's orders, she had gone back to the apartment to shoot him when he came home. But she hadn't been able to do it. Instead, she had vanished, erased herself from Budapest to find a new life and identity. But escape still eluded her.

She felt the morning sun on her back like a brand. The air smelled of metal. Although the night had shown flames in the oil fields, the dawn had changed the scene to dense, billowing clouds of black smoke soaring into the brassy sky. Now and then she heard a grenade explode sharply somewhere in the city. And from across the filthy waters of the harbor she heard the screams of the mob.

The mob of Jidrat was like a resentful animal that had been prodded awake. Sporadic bursts of gunfire came from the white palace, Faiz, the Imam's stronghold on the hill above the city. Captain MacPherson had pointed Faiz out to her as the residence of the Imam Yazid al-Maari. Apparently the royal guards were having trouble with the rioters at the gates. The rifle fire was stitched through with a pattern of bursts from machine guns and grenades. Through the porthole Naomi saw two tanks tumble along the quay and squeeze, like ugly brown beetles, into the narrow streets of the old quarter. They flew the green and white pennons of the Imam's forces. The thud-thud-thud of the cannon followed their disappearance.

Naomi turned away as someone rapped on her cabin door. She drew a deep breath. She did not want to answer it. And then she heard, incredulously, a woman's voice calling her name.

"Miss Haledi?" It was a crisp British accent. "Please let me in. I'm Mrs. Paul Kenton. Are you there? Hurry, please."

Naomi pulled back the bolt and a slender woman in a white suit quickly stepped inside, closed the door, and leaned back against it, staring at her.

"I've come to help you," Esme Kenton said. "There isn't time to explain much. MacPherson came to see me at dawn. To help you. We've decided we can't let Colonel Ta'arife get you, my dear."

"Colonel Ta'arife?"

"Head of the military police. He and the Q'adi started the ball rolling last night, you see. He knows you're aboard. And that you're an Israeli citizen. MacPherson's cabin was forced and his logs were removed last night. Your name and nationality and passport number were logged there, naturally."

"I will be arrested then," Naomi said flatly.

"Yes. As a spy. Do you understand?"

"I have been able to think of nothing else. But why should you help me?"

"Why not? They'll use you, child. If the mob effort slackens and fails, they'll come here for you and stand you up in an open truck and parade you through the city as an enemy tolerated by the Imam."

"How do you know all this?"

"I've lived here a long time. Too long," Esme said bitterly. "You're being held in reserve, child. That's why I've come—while there is still time. I'll get you ashore."

"Ashore? No, no, I couldn't—"

"Safer than on this tub. If you can give Ta'arife the slip for even twenty-four hours, things might straighten out."

Naomi studied Esme Kenton uncertainly. The tall woman looked tense and strained, as if her outwardly calm efficiency was a façade maintained only by a trembling, extraordinary effort.

"You have your own troubles, Mrs. Kenton," Naomi said quietly, astonished at herself for her words. "I could not burden you with mine, too."

"It's my husband," Esme said. "I think they've killed him. He's been missing for three days and I can't get anyone to help me look for him. Nevertheless, I can't let you stay here, child. Do you need to take anything with you? We may be away for two or three days, as I said, until things settle down and some sort of arrangement is made with whoever wins the fighting today."

"I . . . I can go as I am. But are you sure—?"

"It's now or never. While the city is confused."

"All right," Naomi decided suddenly. "I felt so trapped just waiting here, where they knew they could find me. I . . . I'm grateful."

"Just hurry, that's all. We'll stay at the al-Zaysir. It's a ratty hotel and there are only a few foreigners there, but we've all decided it's the best place to hole up until things blow over. The oil people have their own places out in the desert. None of us can get through the roadblocks to join them now, unfortunately. So we stay at the al-Zaysir. All right?"

Naomi managed a tremulous smile and nod. Her fear moved in her and made her physically ill. She conquered it only by a great effort. She felt as if the nightmare that had haunted her since Budapest had at last become real. She could almost feel her flesh being torn apart by the maniacal mob.

Colonel Ta'arife listened for a moment to the noise of the street crowd, and was satisfied. Then he let the Negro slave close the door behind him and ascended the cool, dark stairs to the inner garden of the Q'adi Ghezri's house. It was like stepping into another world: to leave the hot stench of the streets and the screaming, dirty people; to quit the sporadic sounds of gunfire and the wailing of sirens. It had begun! That was the principal thing. The first step was taken. Perhaps a little sooner than planned, but one could not always anticipate the plans of Allah.

His companion, Major Kolia Mikelnikov, had landed safely at the airport and now mounted the steps behind him. Nothing was betrayed on the Russian's long, tired face. The lavish luxury of the Q'adi's quarters, with its garden of jasmine and bougainvillea and the serenity of its softly tinkling fountain, seemed to make no impression on Mikelnikov, whose face was a flat mask, official and unemotional.

The Q'adi stood like a tall black bird of prey upon a cushioned platform at the far end of the garden. On a table nearby were massive, ornately tooled leather-bound volumes of the Koran and the Sunna. A houseboy in a snowy white robe bowed himself away. The Q'adi's long black robe and turban with the band of green that indicated he had made the hadj to Mecca looked like a well of midnight against the ivory carving of a screen behind him. For a moment Ta'arife considered the screen with a certain nervousness, not wishing to be surprised by eavesdroppers or armed men of the Q'adi's. And for another moment doubt shook him—he who was so emancipated from the orthodoxy of Islam—and he wondered if, indeed, this man in black could be the Mahdi, here today to deliver true believers into eternal paradise.

They greeted each other formally with the graceful Arabic salutation of fingers to forehead, lips, and heart.

"This is the man who will help us," Ta'arife said. His narrow face wore a smile. His teeth, under his neat mustache, were shining. "He has just flown in from Baghdad as the head of a mission to cooperate in the delivery of arms, as well as in new engineering projects in the oil fields. He has gone beyond this, Q'adi, with plans for new irrigation developments and all the other matters we have discussed. This is Major Kolia Mikelnikov."

"The desert kites know where the dead have fallen," Ghezri said. "Their flight in the sky, describing great wheels of bad fortune, are always the first sign of a man's death." The hawk face with the great nose and the fanatic eyes regarded Ta'arife angrily. He spoke, then, in Arabic. "He came quickly. Does he understand me?"

"I do," Mikelnikov replied. He smiled and bowed. "I hope to change your impression of me as quickly as possible."

"You came with arms for Islam?"

"A shipment is on its way. We can bring some in by plane. The vessels will arrive in three days."

"But the revolution has begun this morning. The shipment may be too late, if matters go badly for us. We could not wait. We understand that Prince Amr al-Maari is coming back. We must win quickly, or not at all."

"That is understood," Kolia said.

"Colonel Ta'arife has told me your price. The American who will arrive with the prince—he is to be yours."

"With your permission, Q'adi."

"*Billahi!* A man's life is of no importance in the face of the eternities of Allah, Allah be praised."

"Then we are agreed, Q'adi?"

"Let us see how the battle progresses. Come," the Q'adi said.

He led the way behind the screen, where, Ta'arife noted with relief, no one lurked. A balcony yielded a view of Jidrat. The Q'adi's slippered feet made soft, sliding sounds on the tile floor. From the balcony the Q'adi could see the mob rioting in the streets and bazaars. Most of the merchants had been forewarned, and steel shutters guarded their wares, and their baradas were empty.

This quarter of the city—the one nearest the quays and the harbor—was definitely in the hands of the Q'adi's forces, who were dedicated to a new and greater jihad, a holy war to give rebirth to the glory and power of Islam, Allah willing. But the Imam's guards still controlled the hillside approaches to Faiz, the Imam palace. Yet, Ghezri thought, the Imam Yazid is old and weak, lost in the poetry and philosophies of former times. Jidrat was a small nation. Only a tiny seed.

As he watched the smoke rise from the sabotaged oil fields beyond the city, the Q'adi felt within himself the flames of a holy voice, an unquenchable dedication to the cause he was destined to lead. It was regrettable that Colonel Ta'arife— that petty, strutting imitation of other dictators—had to be used, as well as this big, ungainly, sad-eyed foreigner. One shook hands with one's enemies these days and smiled over cups of black coffee and made plans for mutual tasks to be carried out. But when the time came, the Q'adi's voice would cry out from all the minarets in all the mosques of Islam in a sound of thunder that would shake the world. . . .

Colonel Ta'arife studied the same scene and noted with a military eye the movement of the tanks in the narrow streets leading to Faiz. He tried to conceal his worry over the way things were going. The mob in its violence was not violent enough. He knew them. He could play upon the temper of this rabble the way a musician fingers the nuba. He had paid agitators, of course, and other officers had joined the rebellion, seeing in it a chance for personal advancement when the

Imam's palace fell to dust. But the mob was the true implement of revolution. And the mob was a dangerous, two-edged sword. Whip them with words and promises and anger and they responded, screaming, by destroying whatever came in their way. But they had not yet reached the defenses of Faiz and if matters went on much longer, the mob would recoil, frustrated, and with the fickle temper of a headless monster, turn upon those who had called it into being.

Ta'arife knew this must not happen. He still had the Israeli girl. He could take her, when he needed her, and spread the rumor of spies; then exhibit her as fact, a deadly enemy admitted in Jidrat by the senile Imam Yazid. Ta'arife, thinking of this, felt more confident. . . .

Major Mikelnikov was not interested in the current confusion in the city. He had not slept for forty-eight hours, and he knew he needed rest desperately. But he dared not sleep. He had failed twice in his mission. He could not fail again. When he thought of Durell, frustration moved in him and ended his weariness.

Perhaps, he thought, it is because you are not a professional assassin yourself. One can devote a lifetime to intelligence work and feel that the fruits of one's work made some small contribution to the safety of Russia. But to kill a man coldly—not in the heat of war, but by stealth and with snares —this was different. No rationalization could convince him that this shadow war of counter intelligence was the same as the heat of battle.

But Moscow was impatient. So far, he had failed to prevent Durell from contacting the prince. And he had not eliminated Durell. A sorry record, Mikelnikov thought broodingly. And a dangerous one.

A man had his life to lose, if he failed. This was understood. In the Stalinist days, one received short shrift for failure. Today, the agony of the end might be lengthened, even postponed under "humane" punishment. He would be banished to some obscure province, given dull and stultifying work, and worst of all, he would not be able to go on with his search for Naomi, his wife.

If he could see her just once, he thought, and explain how it had happened. Not that it would excuse anything. But if he could just one more time tell her he loved her, beg her forgiveness for what he had done under the implacable pressure of military orders—well, he could die then. To see her face again, as it once had been; to hold her in his arms, as he once had held her—these were dreams, impossible to fulfill. She might be dead. She might be anywhere in the world. Yet he had gone on searching and asking wherever he could, wherever his work took him.

Now he was here, and soon Durell would be here, and it was necessary to kill again. He admired and liked Durell. He would have preferred this man as a friend to all the other men he had ever met. They were alike, perhaps: recognizing each other as an enemy, having suffered the same dangers, the same pangs of conscience, perhaps even the same grief.

Still, Durell had to die.

There was no way out of the trap. It was either Durell or Mikelnikov.

Kolia looked up at the sky. It was just noon.

Chapter Twelve

Sun, sea, and sky coalesced in an inferno of blind white heat. The sea and sky had no end and no beginning. They merged with each other at an indefinable distance, in a melting haze. On the sea, the dhow lifted and fell in the long swells, moving as on hills of oil over the surface of the water. There was nothing to see but the mist, which was like the inside of a furnace. Overhead, there was an aureole of colored light around a hole in the sky where the sun breathed its fiery light upon an empty world.

The nakhoda said, "It is the breath of Allah, effendi. When He so desires, the wind will come again." Abdhuahram was a big man with a weathered face. He was naked to the waist, bearded and wild. As master of the two-masted dhow, he looked as all nakhodas have looked since ancient times. "Yes, the wind will come again, effendi. Perhaps by evening."

"The sooner the better," Durell said.

"It will be according to Allah's mercy. One cannot guess the time it takes for God to destroy that which He has built. He made the sea and sun and the sands of the desert—even the smallest grain—and every drop of water. He made this calm. He will make the wind again."

"You promised it would take only one day to run down the coast to Jidrat."

"Yes, master. If Allah was willing," the nakhoda nodded.

The dhow smelled. It creaked and groaned and plashed against the burning sea. Under the striped cotton awning slung across the cushioned afterdeck, Prince Amr sipped water and fell back, gasping, on his mat. He was naked except for shorts, and his fat, pale body labored to live, sweated and glistened and heaved with each heartbeat, shaking like the fat of a woman's body. The patch of dressing where he had been wounded looked relatively clean. Durell left the taffrail and walked back to him. He squatted in the shade of the canvas. It seemed hotter under the awning.

"How do you feel, Bogo?"

"At the moment, I am happy. And do you know why?"

Amr whispered. "Because I lie here and dream of what I will do to you, Cajun, for bringing me into this. Soon I will have the power of revenge. I was happy where I was. I have no political ambitions. What am I doing on this filthy old vessel, with these filthy men? When I can, Cajun, I will cut out your eyes and your tongue. I will emasculate you. I will—"

"Can I get you anything right now?" Durell asked calmly.

"Reach Death for me, and hand it to me as a gift. Blind me, and wipe this inferno from my sight. I ask you again—what am I doing here?"

"You're going home," Durell said.

"The rebellion has begun. You heard the radio in Karachi yesterday. It is too late."

"Not for you."

"At home they will kill me."

"Not if you stand up to them."

"It is too late for that, too. Too late in time; too late for me. What am I, Cajun? Less than a man, you say. And it is true. Will the people listen to me? You are mad."

"They will follow you if you ask them to."

"I have no wish to be the Imam Amr al-Maari of Jidrat."

"It is your destiny," Durell said.

Amr simply groaned and rolled away from him. Durell lifted his eyes to the horizon. The stony flint and limestone and basaltic cliffs of Southern Arabia hung off the port quarter in the haze of the heat like something dimly seen in a nightmare. He wiped sweat from his face. The dhow rolled and groaned and creaked. The lateen sails flapped. They drifted.

At the huge tiller, Abdhuahram's huge body bowed in drowsiness. Amidships, the ragged, piratical crew of Arab sailors had built a charcoal fire in the huge turtle shell that served as a cooking hearth. The lamb that was still alive made a faint bleating sound, as if it knew it would soon be spitted and roasting over the coals.

Nothing else seemed to live in the sea except the sharks. The sharks followed the dhow in circles, their black, triangular fins cutting through the white haze over the water in lazy, patient patterns.

They had flown to Karachi in Pakistan and then had gone by train and truck to a small port on the eastern shore of the Gulf where sixty miles of brazen sea separated them from Jidrat.

That morning, the radio had been full of conflicting stories of revolt in Jidrat: of looting, and burning, and street fighting; of an assault against Faiz. Zoraya had arranged for the, nakhoda and his dhow, paid for with Durell's American dollars. There was no other safe way to enter Jidrat. The airport would be closed and guarded. It was rumored that a number of Europeans were prisoners in the Hotel al-Zaysir and were being threatened by the howling mobs. But now they had been at sea for hours, and there was no radio aboard, and no news.

Zoraya came out of the cabin shelter. She wore a white blouse and dark skirt and had a ribbon tied in her thick black hair. She looked more English than Arab. Her astonishing amber eyes touched the nakhoda's barbaric figure at the tiller, rested on Amr for a moment, and then looked at Durell. He walked toward her. From amidships came the sudden burst of high, thin quarreling among the crew. Zoraya rested against the taffrail. She looked exhausted.

"Are you all right?" Durell asked.

"I wish you would not be so thoughtful," she said. "It makes it difficult for me."

"Did you sleep?"

"No. Are we near the port?"

"The wind's died. We're drifting." He gestured to the barren cliffs and desert of the shore. Now and then they could hear the thunder of surf on basaltic reefs. It was a dangerous coast. "Have you talked again to Amr?"

She shrugged. "He is full of pity for himself. Nothing I say will make him into the man you wish he was, Durell. I am afraid for you. He talks of vengeance for having his pleasures disturbed. If he lives, he will injure you. If he lives."

"I've brought him this far for him and for his people."

"He needs steel in him, and it is not there. Perhaps it was never there."

"But you remain loyal to him," Durell pointed out.

"Yes, loyal. But loyalty is not love."

"But you still love him."

"I do not know," Zoraya said quietly. "I am confused. The world spins, and I fall with it, and I lose all perspective. I do not know if what you plan for Amr is right. And it may be too late now anyway."

"Zoraya, if you appeared in Jidrat with him—"

"He will not have me at his side."

"But if you could persuade him, the people would support him. We need this."

"We?"

Durell said flatly, "Jidrat is as much a part of the world struggle as any other place on earth. At the moment, it is more important than most. Tomorrow, perhaps, it will be forgotten."

"Yes. If Amr is killed."

"Talk to him, Zoraya. Try to make him listen to you."

"It is no use."

"You must try," Durell said.

She went across the deck and sat beside Amr under the awning, and began to talk to him. He would not look at her. He smoked one of Abdhuahram's narghiles and watched the sea. After a time she got up and stood alone, watching the sharks that circled the boat.

At two o'clock the wind was still dead. The dhow drifted closer to shore, and the roar of the surf was louder, and the spume of the breakers was visible. The crew finished eating and watched the shore worriedly. The nakhoda stood like a giant idol at the tiller, motionless. Zoraya again sat in silence beside Amr.

Durell was the first to hear the beat of the other vessel's motor. There was a thin heat mist over the oily sea, and nothing could be seen. Then the nakhoda heard the sound and issued a sharp, brief command to his Arab sailors. They stirred uneasily. Then, out of the heat mist, there appeared another dhow—diesel-driven, sails furled, a white curl of foam at its high bow.

At the same time the air carried with it the smell of the other vessel. It was a smell Durell thought unknown in this century: the smell of many human bodies penned below the decks in a filthy sailing vessel. Chained in miserable slavery. Abdhuahram reached for a polished ram's horn and blew a series of curious blasts that carried sharply across the water. The second dhow fell to drifting, fifty feet off the port side.

Durell crossed to the giant nakhoda. "Are they slavers?"

"We do not question them, effendi. The captain is my brother." Abdhuahram grinned and tugged at his barbaric beard. "The traffic is legal here in Jidratti territorial waters. He will help us. He will take us to the village of the Al Murra, the tribe of our fathers. He unloads his cargo there.

You will see and remember nothing of this, naturally."

Durell watched the second dhow drift alongside. A line was snaked from one vessel to the other. The stench of the slaver was overpowering in the heat. A constant wail of misery came from the other ship. Zoraya stood beside Durell. Her lips were pale.

"I am sorry this has to be seen."

"I know that slavery exists here," Durell said.

"We have tried to abolish it, but it is a lucrative business. The tribal sheiks inland, who have no oil holdings, would rebel if they could not act as middlemen in the slave traffic."

The towline was made fast, and the slaver proceeded. Motion was resumed at last off the barren coast. In twenty minutes the shoreline changed, became indented with rocky coves that were terminal points for deeply gullied wadis carved in the face of the cliffs. Amr stirred himself and began to talk in undertones to the nakhoda. Durell noted that the nakhoda's replies were prompt and respectful. The Prince of Jidrat then came across the hot deck to join Durell and Zoraya.

"We will go ashore in a few minutes," Amr said. "The village of Al Murra is the terminus for the usual caravan route across the Rub 'al Khali to Riyadh, in Saudi Arabia. Nowadays, trucks are used instead of camels, so there will be transportation for us. It is only another twenty minutes to Jidrat from Al Murra. There will be no difficulty, once we are ashore —unless, of course, the local sheik becomes alarmed at having Western eyes see his business. Lately, there has been some sensitivity about it."

"The nakhoda seems to be your man," Durell said. "Are the Al Murra tribesmen also loyal to you, Amr?"

Amr smiled strangely. "I had almost forgotten what it was like, this blind obedience. When we are ashore, Durell, you will no longer be in command. I shall give the orders."

"As you say."

"And it is possible," Amr said slyly, "that I may order your death."

"I'll take that chance."

"I have no reason to love you, you know. But I shall decide your fate later. Now we must land."

There was no dock or harbor that Durell could see. Only a cove with a wadi reaching inland beyond it; a tumbled waste of rock and sand in the blinding afternoon heat. Combers crashed and battered against the nearby shore, and there was

a long line of spume betraying a reef across the mouth of the
cove. The towline snapped taut as the slaver dhow increased
speed. The deck lurched uneasily. The high prow swung
around in the slaver's wake and Durell saw an opening in the
basalt reef ahead, wide enough for the boats to run through.
The passage was quick, expertly made. Ahead, to the left of
the wadi entrance, was a beach of stony shingle. They entered between the jaws of the red sandstone cliffs. It was like
entering the mouth of a furnace. From the slaver dhow came
wails of muffled terror.

The nakhoda ran forward, beating at his men with a small
thonged whip, and drove them to cast off the towline. Then
he ran back—a giant panting figure—and lurched against the
sweep of the tiller. Their vessel slowly swung out of the
slaver's wake. The other dhow, engine-driven, backed off and
lost way, but their own vessel had no such control. It surged
toward the beach, lifting in high swells that quickened by the
moment. A comber crashed, burst, heeled them over. They
threatened to broach to in the surf.

"Ya Allah!" Abdhuahram grunted. The muscles rippled,
crawled, and bunched along his giant torso. The mast
creaked. The tattered sails broke loose and fell in a tumble
of salt-stiffened canvas. The next moment the deck trembled
as the keel ground into the stony beach. There were two more
jolts, a long, groaning noise, and then they came to rest.

Durell helped Zoraya ashore. Amr ignored her. They waded
through lime-green tepid water, waist-deep, some distance
from where the slaver dhow had moored just outside the line
of breakers. There were calls and shouts and jeering com-
ments from one crew to the other. Durell struggled out of
the surf, helping Zoraya, and then saw Prince Amr coming
ashore. He rode astride Abdhuahram's giant shoulders as if
the nakhoda was nothing more than a beast of burden.

In a matter of moments they were all ashore.

The heat struck at them. Silence surrounded them.

Durell saw the nakhoda uneasily survey the barren, rocky
scarp surrounding the cove. Sweat poured off them. Heat
rolled down from the cliffs like a waterfall. Nothing stirred.
The air tasted metallic. The second dhow rolled offshore, her
engine idling.

Abdhuahram grunted. "This is the meeting place. I am
sure my brothers of the Al Murra are here. But why do they
not show themselves?"

"Perhaps because of me," Durell said.

"Or the woman."

Durell looked at Zoraya. She had walked over to the shadow of a giant black boulder and was standing there. Amr was with her, surprisingly. Then Abdhuahram gripped Durell's forearm with strong brown fingers.

"There. There are the Al Murra."

Silently, almost furtively, like a pack of ragged hunting dogs, the tribesmen appeared; first one, then two, then more, leaping and sliding down the face of the cliffs by way of a dozen faint paths. Most of them wore tattered turbans of rags over their shoulder-length, greasy black hair. They wore skirts and sandals and dirty robes. A few had old British Army berets. They were armed with all sorts of weapons—from long-barreled rifles to Sten guns. All had knives tucked in their belts. They looked wild and barbaric and dangerous and unpredictable as they streamed in thickening numbers from the mouth of the wadi.

"No man can tell what the Al Murra will do," murmured the nakhoda. "Do not move. Are you afraid?"

"Not yet," Durell replied.

"It would be wise if you were."

Now there was a shout from the slaver dhow and a quick, ululating response from the Al Murra. Someone fired a rifle into the air. The single sharp report echoed back and forth in the cup of intolerable heat between the red sandstone cliffs. From up in the wadi came the grinding sound of a truck's motor starting, and then several old vehicles appeared, bumping and rocking over the ground. They were obviously going to load up with the slaves—poor devils transported by treachery and greed from the African Sudan and the Sahara.

From the first truck came a wild shout, and the vehicle rocketed across the beach toward them. From the cab jumped two armed men who shouted a challenge to the nakhoda. Then a third man with a white beard and an immaculate white robe stepped down. The old man was obviously the sheik of the tribesmen. He stared at Durell and rapped a gutteral question at Abdhuahram, who, for all his giant strength, seemed suddenly servile and anxious to please. The nakhoda fell to his knees, pointed to the stout figure of Prince Amr, said his name, and bowed his head in the dust.

There was an abrupt silence.

The tribesmen turned and stared at the prince.

The old man sucked in a deep breath of surprise and

walked around the prostrate figure of the nakhoda to the prince. To Durell, it seemed as if Amr, the young man he had known at Yale so long ago, struggled to emerge, in this distant barren place, from under the fat of dissipation. The prince seemed to stand straighter and taller for a moment as the old white-bearded sheik salaamed and murmured the age-old Arabic greeting.

"Wallahi! Peace, by the mercy of Allah."

"And to you, friend of my father," Amr said.

"Ibn Ibrahim remembers his sworn oath," said the old man. "Command us, and we follow you."

"In a moment," Amr said.

Again there was a subtle change in the atmosphere on the sun-baked beach. A hail came from the slaver dhow offshore. Ibn Ibrahim made a quick inquiry of the prince. Amr nodded. A hatch was opened, and curses and yelps followed sharp orders hurled at the unfortunates below. In a moment, a thin stream of black and brown men, women, and children climbed miserably to the dhow's deck, staggering in their rags, dazed and crushed by the afternoon sun.

Durell turned as Amr walked across the shingle toward him. The Al Murra—wild and eager—ringed him in with their varied weapons. A sharp word from the white-bearded Ibrahim brought half a dozen of the fellows closer, grinning. Their teeth were irregular; worn and broken, with many gaps. They suffered from trachoma, and there was more than one blind white eye among them. Their lank, greasy hair hung in long curls from under the rags of their turbans. But for all that, they were tough and wiry men, reckless of human life.

"Cajun, we are now in my country," Amr said. "Do you remember what I promised you. You did not choose to believe my demand for revenge. I did not want to come back. You forced me to come here."

"You would have been killed, on Elba."

"But I was not. You took advantage of my temporary panic. You forced me to return. But now the tables are turned, eh? You gambled on the wrong hand, you see. We do not play poker now. The game we play is watched by the whole world. You may think I am a poor specimen of a man, but here I am important, and I know the importance of Jidrat. Yes, you have bet on the wrong side."

"Tell me plainly what you mean, Amr."

"You brought me back to use me for Washington's purposes, yes? However, I have always preferred to make my own choice in such matters. I have been told that revolution began in Jidrat today."

"Yes."

"You want me to control this thing and follow your suggestions?"

"Just do what you think is right, Amr," Durell said. "You know what that is."

"Do I? I am a reprobate, a debaucher of women, a drug addict, a besotted pleasure-hunter."

"That's not all of it."

"No. But the whole world thinks that. And so do you. Do not lie to me. I promised I would revenge myself for your behavior toward me. Toward my royal person. As my first act, I arrest you as an enemy of the state."

"Don't be a fool," Durell said.

Prince Amr slapped him. There was a murmur, like a shock wave, from the tribesman. A tall, hawk-nosed fellow stepped forward, lifted his rifle butt as if to brain Durell. Zoraya cried out. The prince looked at her and laughed.

"Your turn will come later. I am sick of you. Sick of your following me, sick of your advice and hopes for me." He turned and gave an order to the eager tribesmen. Durell felt someone wrench his arm from behind. He began to struggle, then checked himself. It was useless to fight back now. There were too many of them. And there was nowhere to go, even if he could escape. He looked at Amr and saw all the sly evil, all the perverse cruelty in the man.

It seemed to Durell, in that moment, that he had made his last and greatest mistake.

Zoraya cried out again. He tried to duck away from the Al Murra who swung at him with the rifle butt, but he was held too tightly to escape. The weapon crashed against his shoulder and he fell to his knees. He tried to rise again. Through a dancing haze he saw Prince Amr grinning at him. The man's face was twisted in vengeful triumph. Then another blow landed on the back of Durell's neck. He fell forward, feeling the scorching heat of the flinty beach under his hands.

And then everything whirled away into darkness.

Chapter Thirteen

THE ROOM at the Hotel al-Zaysir was hot and airless. Esme Kenton stood at the window and stared at the Israeli girl on the bed. Naomi was asleep. It seemed to Esme that only deep physical and spiritual exhaustion could enable anyone to sleep here now. But she was glad Naomi was getting rest. The girl would need strength later, and the less chance she had to think about the immediate future, the better.

Esme wished for Paul with a dull, aching longing. It was so difficult to go through these hours without him. It was as if a part of her had suddenly been amputated. She missed him and feared for him, and she told herself he could not be dead. Yet she knew there was little hope. Too much time had passed without word from him. If he were lost in the desert, the sun would have killed him by now. If a disabling sandstorm had stranded him somewhere, well, he might still be alive, but only if he had been prepared for it.

The thud-thud of mortar shells bracketing an Army post below Faiz made her turn back to the window. The afternoon was waning. The sky looked ocherous and there was an unhealthy haze that made the sun a huge glowing spot in the western heavens. The day's fighting was confused. Nobody in the hotel knew what was happening. Even T. P. Fenner, the American consul, who'd been trapped here since early morning, knew it was too dangerous at this moment for any Westerner to appear on the streets of Jidrat.

Paul, she cried soundlessly. *Paul, where are you?*

The only others in the hotel were a few servants, a Greek couple, two Indian businessmen from Bombay, and an Argentinean. Captain MacPherson was in the bar with Fenner now. At noon, an Army captain with a squad of excited rebel soldiers had posted themselves in the lobby. All foreigners were to stay indoors. Further orders would come when the situation was clarified.

The al-Zaysir had been built at the turn of the century, when the English established a protectorate under the Imam Yazid. The hotel was a short distance away from a central

111

bazaar area. From the hotel's flat roof, equipped with tables and awnings for the European guests, one could see the harbor and the surrounding stone hills of the desert and the looming *djebels* of the interior. There were accommodations for only twenty guests.

Esme suddenly remembered the Russian, Major Mikelnikov, who had checked in while Naomi was sleeping. The Russian had arrived with Ta'arife, which surely meant that the hotel was safe. But then he'd gone out again immediately with the colonel. Apparently, Esme thought, the restrictions against foreigners did not apply to *him*.

The sudden crack of an exploding grenade made dust jump from the ceiling. Naomi's face had been relaxed in sleep, but with the sudden explosion her features convulsed and she sat up with a little cry of fear. Her eyes were still closed. Her dark hair was plastered to her cheek in damp curls. Then, still sleeping, she turned over again on the bed.

A machine gun chattered. The sky beyond the window was black with oily smoke from the burning storage tanks. There was a quick, soft rapping on the louvered hall door.

Esme turned quickly and crossed the tile floor. They were on the second floor and there had been no alarm from the lobby, where most of the guests had gathered. She had no fear when she opened the door.

"Oh, it's you, Messaoud."

The man was the al-Zaysir's bartender. He had often served Paul and her. He had untidy hair and an oddly dirty, white mess jacket.

He spoke haltingly. "Mrs. Kenton, I am your servant."

"What do you want, Messaoud?"

The man looked at the sleeping girl on the bed and pulled at his long nose. He shrugged. "I have been sent for you. . . . To take you to your husband, lady."

His words struck her like a blow under the ribs. She felt a surge of shuddering hope that was unbearable. "My husband? Paul? You know him? Of course you know him! Is he alive?"

"Yes, Mrs. Kenton."

"Oh, you must be lying," she whispered.

"As Allah is my witness, I have just left him." Messaoud brushed a finger under his long nose. "It is dangerous on the streets, but I have the red truck—the Ford he always uses. You see? I am to drive you to him."

"Where? In the city?"

"No, lady. But it is not far. Just a little bit beyond."

Messaoud looked different somehow. Perhaps it was just the excitement of the street fighting that made him seem strange. He had remarkably thick brows, she thought. He licked his lips and watched her.

"You are to pay me one hundred American dollars," he said.

"One hundred—" Esme halted. "That's ridiculous. I haven't that much with me here. Certainly not today."

"How much do you have?" he asked bluntly.

She turned away, uncertain. Naomi Haledi still slept. It was just as well. She felt a tremor of insane hope that made her want to thrust everything into the Arab's long, narrow hand. She found ten pounds and several rupee notes in her bag. It was all she had—except for the little pearl-handled .28 revolver that Paul had given her long ago; long ago, in another lifetime . . . in Yucatan, she remembered. She did not let Messaoud see the gun. She felt safer for having it.

"Here," she said, thrusting the money at him. "All I have."

The Arab took it silently. He looked at the sleeping Naomi. "Your friend can come with us," he said suddenly.

"No, she must stay. Those are our orders." Esme felt suspicion strike her. "How is it you know about my husband and have his truck? How is it you can take me to him?"

"It will be dangerous, lady." Messaoud smirked. "But I know ways out of the city that will not be guarded."

"Just tell me if he is well," Esme begged.

"Oh, yes, lady. Very well."

"Then let's go before she wakes," Esme said, with a nod toward Naomi.

Messaoud nodded and went out. He did not look back to see if she followed. She hesitated, her heart pounding. Should she wake up Naomi anyway? The girl ought to be told something. Esme herself didn't know whether she would return to the al-Zaysir, or stay with Paul, or what. There were other questions she wanted to ask, but Messaoud was already trotting down the back steps at the far end of the silent, hot corridor. A grenade blasted spitefully in the bazaar several streets away. It was clear that Messaoud would not wait for more questions. And after all, he was the bartender here, he had always been courteous, she and Paul knew him well.

She turned and ran down the hall to the stairs.

The hotel was so sparsely occupied that she met no one.

The soldiers and other guests were all in the front lobby. Messaoud beckoned from the kitchen door, and she went that way.

"Wait a moment. Please. Can't you tell me anything more?"

"There is no time, lady," Messaoud said. "It is dangerous to wait. I was told to fetch you. That is all I can tell."

She followed the tall Arab through the deserted, evil-smelling hotel kitchen and out through a back passage into a narrow alley. A flight of stone steps led up into an archway in a strip of sunlight. A thin dog slunk out of their way. She hurried, stumbling to keep up with Messaoud.

"Come. This way."

They went through a doorway and across a single room furnished with a primus stove, a rickety table, some wooden chairs, and two prayer rugs. Then down a hall and out through another doorway into the next street. Somewhere a baby wailed. There was no one in sight.

It would be all right, she told herself. Why should anyone trick her? Anyway, she had the gun in her purse. And Messaoud, for all his evil appearance, was certainly harmless and anxious to help.

She saw the battered red Ford truck with another renewal of hope. Yes, it was Paul's! It was parked in front of a shop that was shuttered in steel. The whole city seemed to be dead. The silence was ominous. The street was just wide enough for the pickup truck to squeeze between the blank walls of the native houses with their balconies that leaned and almost touched overhead. She squirmed into the cab with Messaoud.

"What about the troops and tanks on patrol?" she asked.

"They are attacking Faiz, the Imam's palace. We will be safe."

Messaoud paused to throw a dirty white *galibaya* over his mess jacket. The transformation was instant and complete when he added a rag of a headcloth. He looked like any other street Arab then.

He started off with a rush, driving recklessly around corners without slowing at all. Esme had no chance to ask more questions. The ride was too hazardous to allow her anything beyond her sense of immediate jeopardy. Now and then thick acrid smoke billowed down from the burning oil tanks and set her to coughing.

Once they almost ran head-on into the rear of a parked medium-weight tank. It was shelling a house down the street that had sandbag parapets on the roof. The green pennon of the Imam snapped off the tank's radio aerial. The cannon made sharp cracking noises. The wind was hot and ashen. Plaster and wood burst from a corner of the beseiged building, and screaming began inside. Messaoud quickly backed up and they took another street before the tank's crew even noticed them.

Several bodies lay sprawled in the next street. Messaoud ran over them, careless in noting whether the fluttering white robes covered dead men or only wounded. The truck lurched, bounced. A shop burned nearby, and then rubble blocked the next intersection. Messaoud muttered thinly under his breath and made another detour.

After fifteen minutes they reached the boulevard built by the Americans to get to the oil fields. The little truck bounced crazily onto the smooth pavement. The palm trees here looked as if they had been shredded by a giant grinder. A great many more bodies lay strewn like heaps of rags along the sidewalks and in front of the shops.

"We'll be caught in the open like this," Esme protested. "Please. Is it much further? Perhaps we'd better go back. I . . . I feel ill."

"Your husband waits for you, Mrs. Kenton."

"I'm not so sure of that now," Esme said.

"As Allah is my witness—"

"Yes, I know. All right."

They drove west for a mile on the ghostly boulevard. Then Messaoud turned into a small track that led through thinning houses and suddenly out into the flinty desert. The truck bounced and threatened to come apart on the rough road. It could hardly be called a road, Esme thought dimly as she hung on. But no matter. She was going to Paul! She would see him soon. It would be all right. Everything would be all right.

She could not guess their destination. The city was behind and below them. The burnished sea vanished as they crossed a narrow wadi between red cliffs, then cut across a flinty plateau, and then were into another wadi that twisted north.

Messaoud began to sing to himself in a strange dialect as he drove. She could not understand the words, but the man's voice was high and unnatural and unearthly.

"Will we be there soon?" she asked.

He did not reply. He kept on singing.

They came at last to the foot of a high scarp of limestone that formed an irregular bowl of cliffs around them. Esme had the vague idea that they had circled in the desert and come upon Ain Gemilha, the site of Paul's dig, from the side opposite the one by which she usually approached. But she wasn't sure. Messaoud stopped the truck. Dust boiled around them. The sun was hidden behind the high cliffs. In the shadows, the air smelled brassy, like the inside of a furnace.

"We go up. Come," said Messaoud.

She climbed out of the cab and looked about. "Are we so far from Ain Gemilha, Messaoud?"

"Not so far, lady. We come by back way."

She nodded, pleased that her sense of direction had been true. But before she could ask anything more, Messaoud started off—a scarecrow figure, his white robe flapping around his bartender's drill trousers. When his robe flapped open in the exertion of climbing, she saw that his trousers were held up by a strip of rope braided with red string, and that under his mess jacket was the tail of a striped shirt. He looked pathetic and ludicrous, with his bushy mustache in imitation of Kassim and his long, unhealthy nose. He ran across the flint with his big feet slapping dust and then turned up a narrow path angling across the face of the nearest cliff.

Esme hurried into the crushing heat that was trapped beneath the cliffs. Thank God, soon it would be evening and the temperature would drop, she thought. Better the freezing cold of desert night than this suffocating heat. Though it was really six of one, half-dozen of the other, she mused.

Messaoud hurried as if someone snapped at his heels. Esme stumbled, lost a sandal, paused to retrieve it. She was surprised at the height she had already climbed above the wadi floor. The truck looked small, lost in the shadows below. A lizard scuttled away as she picked up her shoe, and she called out while she struggled to replace the sandal.

"Wait for me!"

Her voice echoed erratically. But Messaoud hurried on. She thought she heard his laughter in quick, high, snorting sounds.

She wore a white linen skirt, a blouse, and a short, linen bolero jacket. A blue ribbon tied up her ash-blonde hair. She suddenly thought: I must look a perfect fright. What will Paul think of me, stumbling along after this Arab? No sleep for two nights, worried sick, and now this mad chase after the al-Zaysir's bartender here in the middle of absolute nowhere!

For the first time since Paul had been gone, her relief gave way to a natural resentment against him for frightening her like this with his absence.

The path turned abruptly just below the top of the cliff. Messaoud blocked her way, facing her. He was motionless, his narrow head lowered between his thin shoulders.

"We are here, Mrs. Kenton. Your husband is in the cave."

She saw a dark fissure in the red rock beyond him. The path widened to quite a ledge here.

"Let me by then," she said.

She squeezed past, smelling the acrid odor of his sweat. She suddenly wondered how Messaoud, a Moslem, could work in a bar. A good Moslem never touched liquor. Not to drink it, anyway. But she supposed it was all right for him to serve it to others.

The cave entrance was dark and narrow, but she saw the glare of a gasoline lantern far inside. Sudden apprehension squeezed her heart. Then, before she could turn, a second Arab appeared in the cave entrance. A short man with an enormous belly and thickened legs that indicated some advanced kidney or circulatory disease. He walked toward her with a waddling gait. He wore pantaloons of striped cotton, sneakers, and a striped shirt like Messaoud's. He was completely bald. He carried a new automatic rifle so recently uncrated that its packing grease was not yet completely wiped away. A bandolier of extra cartridges was slung over the man's fat shoulders.

She called past him. "Paul? Paul, are you there?"

Her voice sounded high and frightened and lonely.

Something thrust rudely into the small of her back, pushing her forward. She fell against the fat Arab. He giggled, and Messaoud snorted. It was Messaoud who had pushed her into the cave.

Before she could protest, Messaoud said, "Go see your husband, Englisi lady. Look long on him, and speak to him."

Esme drew a deep breath and walked into the cave.

There was a smell of excrement and urine, of stale food and charred ashes and something indefinable. There were half a dozen pallets against the wall on this side of the gasoline lantern that hissed and sputtered on an old wooden table. Two empty ammunition boxes served as chairs. She saw no one except Messaoud and his fat, giggling friend. They were silent now, and she turned to look at them. Their faces were sharply expectant. Messaoud grinned. The other man nodded his bald head. They were encouraging her to go on, beyond the pool of bright light.

"Paul?" she called again.

Her voice echoed queerly. She clutched her handbag and walked around the table and then could see beyond the lantern's glare.

And she saw Paul, her husband.

He was spread-eagled—naked—on the floor. There were strange designs carved on the thinly muscled skin of his chest and belly. Blood had dried and run and dried again in a tracery of darkness. There was a pool of blood between his legs, and she couldn't look there. She looked at his face. He was dead, she thought. His eyes were closed and his mouth was open and his tongue showed between his teeth in the way of a dead man.

Then he breathed and turned his face toward her and opened his eyes. One of his ears had been sliced off. It looked odd, she thought; just that dark little hole in the side of his head.

Then he said in a grating voice, "Oh my God, Esme."

She wanted to faint, to blot out the unreal sight of him as a horror too great to look upon. She swayed on her feet. But she could not faint. She could not erase his image. And from behind her came Messaoud's thin giggle.

"Your husband will not speak to us, Mrs. Kenton. These are his first words since he became our guest."

She heard Messaoud without really understanding what he said. She could not tear her eyes away from Paul—so impossibly spread-eagled, wrists and ankles tied to stakes in the dirt floor of the cave. He had closed his eyes. He wasn't shaved, and his beard looked thick, shot through with a gray she had never seen there before. The dark shadows made his face look gaunt and hollow. She saw his throat move spasmodically when he swallowed. She dropped to her knees beside him.

"Paul. Paul." She wanted to scream. "What is happening?"

"O God . . . I'm prisoner . . . sorry."

"Why? Why?"

"Blaney."

"Because of Blaney?" It made no sense to her. The name was something out of the past, almost forgotten. Then she remembered. "Oh. You mean John Blaney. The American. The economic specialist—"

"Not economist. . . . Spy," Paul whispered. "They . . . killed him. Messaoud . . . and pals. Listen, Esme. It hurts. I can't—"

"Please, Paul."

"Found out why . . . John killed. . . . Hid something. They want to know. . . . Messaoud . . . takes orders from Colonel Ta'arife."

She felt as if she were going insane. "Ta'arife? He was here? He did this? But he's been to our house for dinner so many—"

"Yes."

"Paul, I . . . I'm going to be sick." She watched him swallow air painfully. She whispered, shuddering, "Will they . . . like John. . . .?"

"They . . . kill me."

"Paul, no!"

"Think so."

"Why not tell them what they want to know?" she cried. He shook his head. "I'm here now, Paul. Will they kill me, too?"

"Don't know. . . . Oh God, Esme . . . they'll try to make me talk . . . by doing things to you," he gasped.

A rough hand suddenly pulled at her shoulder, and she turned, twisting on her knees. Her heart lurched. She shook all over. Messaoud grinned above her. All at once she remembered the tiny gun in her purse. The purse was still clutched in her hand. She knew how to use the gun. Wild hope made her heart thunder in her ears.

She looked at Paul. His eyes were closed. She couldn't tear her eyes away from the dark hole in the side of his head where his ear had been. There was a look of death on his face. A look of finality. She saw the way someone—Messaoud who had mixed drinks for them at the al-Zaysir?—had carved with the tip of a very sharp knife the strange cabalistic signs on Paul's body. She saw that two of the fingers of his left hand had been cut off. His wedding ring—of heavy gold—was gone. Who had it? Messaoud? And what had they done with Paul's fingers?

She felt as if she were going mad.

She began to shake, and that was no good because she

couldn't get the gun from her purse if she weren't quick and nimble. But she couldn't stop shaking. Messaoud, who had wrenched her about as she knelt beside Paul, grinned down at her.

"You will talk more with your husband, lady. We must know where the Q'adi Ghezri hid his secret supply of weapons."

"Weapons?"

"Your husband understands. First Blaney found them, and the Q'adi had him murdered. Then your husband was foolish enough to inquire into it. He knows, Englisi lady. We must learn where the Q'adi hides the weapons he will use against the loyal Army."

"You mean against Colonel Ta'arife?"

"Yes, lady. We are all loyal patriots." Messaoud laughed. "Jidrat for the Jidratti. Down with the Western imperialists. Throw out the capitalist bloodsuckers."

The fat Arab giggled like a woman. Messaoud blew his nose, and Esme shrank back instinctively. The Arab with the enormous paunch said something in a dialect she could not understand. He had a thin knife in his hand. So he was the one who had done those terrible things to Paul! She would shoot him first. Then Messaoud. Then she would get Paul away from here, to a doctor, a hospital—

Messaoud slapped her. The blow knocked her backward—stunned—across Paul. Her weight was hurled against his wounds, and he screamed.

It was Paul's scream of wild hurt that made her act too soon.

She had dropped the purse. She looked for it and it was within easy reach. She picked it up, trying to make the move seem like a vague, feminine gesture. Her blue hair ribbon was loose and her hair screened her face. She had trouble breathing. It was as if something squeezed the air out of her lungs. And she felt dizzy. But she had the purse! She felt the reassuring weight of the gun through the thin linen.

Now! she thought.

She knelt and Messaoud cursed her in shrill Arabic. She opened the purse as she crouched over it, holding it against her stomach, and she reached inside for the little .28. Her hands felt enormous and clumsy. Something struck her in the back as she took out the gun; a tremendous blow that sent her sprawling. The gun flew from her fingers. She realized dimly that she had been kicked. The pain was agonizing.

The contents of her purse spilled over the cave floor: compact, lipstick, coin purse, handkerchief, and gun.

The gun glittered in the light of the hissing lantern.

The fat Arab chattered in warning. She tried to snatch up the gun, but Messaoud ground his heel on her fingers as they closed convulsively over it. Pain shot up her wrist and shoulder and wrenched at her stomach. She screamed. He removed his foot and kicked the gun out of reach—under the table, where he ignored it. Then he leaned down and twisted his fingers in her long hair and yanked her head back until her throat was exposed, taut and straining.

"You try trick on Messaoud?"

She was strangling. She wanted to die with the agony of her failure. She had been so incompetent, so useless in her trying to help Paul.

And now they were doomed.

Messaoud flung her away. She fell and gasped and forced air past the agony in her throat. Messaoud and his fat friend began to argue in quick low voices. Esme looked up and saw that Paul watched her. His smile was thin, his whisper hoarse and painful.

"Good try . . . darling."

"Please, Paul. I muffed it. For my sake, Paul, tell them what they want to know."

"Too many . . . get killed . . . if I do."

"I don't care about that. I love you, darling. I want to go on living, the way it has been. Please tell Messaoud what he wants to know. Tell him for me, Paul. Please."

He shook his head slowly. "Can't," he whispered.

"Paul, darling, Paul—"

"My . . . job," he said finally.

"Job? Job?" she whispered wildly. "But you're a scientist, an archeologist. You're interested in history, in the dead and safe and ancient past. Politics has nothing to do with you."

He nodded. "Yes . . . my job. My real job."

She stared at the tortured figure of her husband. "What? What are you saying?"

"My work here . . . Ain Gemilha . . . legitimate, yes. But a year ago . . . approached by Foreign Office. Working for them ever since. General reports. . . . Pretty useless stuff. Until I began with Blaney . . . here in Jidrat. . . ." His voice trailed away.

"You really worked with John?" she insisted.

He nodded painfully. "Then they . . . killed him. The

Q'adi. Holding out against Ta'arife." His voice strengthened for a moment. "Now Ta'arife and his new Brotherhood . . . desperate to find Ghezri's ace-in-the-hole."

"Then tell them," she said urgently. "Tell them, please, and they'll let us go."

"No," he whispered.

"But why not? We couldn't harm them."

"Yes . . . we could. We know about it, you see? So . . . it would be useless." He stared at her with tormented eyes. His breathing was raw. "You don't really . . . want me to tell them . . . now, Es, do you?"

"I'm a coward. You're more important than anything else in the world, darling. I'm not afraid for myself. . . . Well, maybe I am. No false heroics, Paul. I'm shaking with fear. But it's you, Paul. Duty makes demands and all that, yes, but—"

"Wouldn't save us," he whispered. "Messaoud coming. . . ."

Messaoud reached down and flung her away from Paul's naked body. He held her with his left hand and carried a knife in his right. The other Arab squatted and watched with bright eyes. Messaoud asked Paul a question. Paul shook his head. Messaoud kicked him and screamed at him again. Paul gave no answer. Suddenly Messaoud plunged the knife into the upper part of Paul's thigh and dragged it down through the flesh. It seemed to Esme she could hear the blade scrape bone. Blood spurted. Messaoud pulled out the knife and asked his question again. The fat Arab laughed.

Esme wanted to faint, but a scream came from her throat instead.

Messaoud turned to her, his eyes wide, unblinking. It was incredible to think that she had once known this man as a rather awkward waiter and bartender in the Hotel al-Zaysir. He said, "You will persuade your husband, Mrs. Kenton."

"No," she whispered.

He reached out, and caught the neck of her blouse and ripped it open. She tried to tear herself away, but he fell on top of her and tore off her skirt and then her brassiere. The fat Arab stood up, his face all at once gone soft and silent and waiting. Esme felt Messaoud's hands roughly searching her body.

"Stand up, Englisi lady."

She got to her feet—naked—before the two Arabs. It didn't matter. Their eyes searched her body, lingering with interest. She didn't look at Paul. She didn't know if he was still alive or not.

Messaoud slowly and deliberately took off his clothes and stood as naked as she. His body was thin and bony and angular, marked with sores. He came toward her and when she tried, suddenly, to run around the table, he caught her and threw her hard against the rock wall of the cave. An acid taste rose in her throat. She felt his weight fall on her and smelled his fetid breath as he gasped excitedly. The other Arab said something in a shrill voice. Esme tried to turn her head aside. She could see the entrance to the cave. It was dark. When had night come?

She bit off her screams when Messaoud was deliberately cruel. She felt crushed, smothered, suffocated under his dirtiness. The Arab smelled of grease and sweat. She tried to bite his throat. Her teeth caught his skin and came away with a small piece of flesh. Messaoud did not seem to feel it. But then, suddenly, the fat Arab shouted a warning and Messaoud lifted up from her and she saw that Paul had somehow gotten one wrist free of the stakes that tied him to the cave floor. He had scrabbled in the dirt and found a shard of flint, and he threw this at Messaoud.

It caught Messaoud in the left eye with a strange, wet, smacking sound and Esme saw Messaoud's eye, torn partly from its socket by the jagged flint. Messaoud screamed and sprang up and snatched at his knife. Paul tried to get his other wrist free, but Messaoud jumped on him and the fat Arab sat on Paul's head and chest and Messaoud began driving the knife into Paul's body—first here and then there —with quick, punching gestures. Blood streamed down Messaoud's face from his torn eye that hung against his cheek. Paul's long white legs jerked and quivered. Blood ran over the floor. Messaoud kept driving the knife into Paul's body over and over again. And then Esme saw Paul's legs stop moving, and she knew he was dead.

After a while, the fat Arab got up and threw himself on her. She tried to fight him off. But it it was useless.

What followed seemed to go on for hours.

One small part of her mind floated in detachment and wondered that the night was so dark and starless.

Chapter Fourteen

DURELL was aware, first, of the chill bite of the night air in the desert. Then he listened to the peculiar stillness. The truck into which he had been thrown by the Al Murra people, who had bound him hand and foot, had come to a grinding halt. For several hours, it seemed, since he had been beaten unconscious on the beach, they had travelled in irregular fits and starts. The journey, in company with three other trucks, was a slow and jolting one that followed no special road that he could determine. Nor was there much he could see. By straining awkwardly, he had been able to look out through the underside of the flapping truck canvas. But there was nothing except the desert, obscured by dust, and an occasional glimpse of a tribesman trotting alongside the slowly jolting, grinding vehicle which went no faster than a man could walk.

Other armed men had sat on the tail gate of Durell's truck. He did not know what had happened to Zoraya and Prince Amr. They were up front, he supposed, with Ibn Ibrahim, the old sheik. All he had been able to do, when he revived, was make himself comfortable and wait for the trip to end.

Now the truck had halted. He did not think it was because they had reached any special destination. The armed men on the tail gate had jumped off and run away somewhere, and he could hear their thick, gutteral voices in argument about something. He gathered that one of the trucks had broken down and that there was some question about the wisdom of going on—immediately, anyway. A storm was coming.

Durell rolled over and sat up. His hands were tied behind his back; his ankles were lashed with a leather thong. His head ached. He was as thirsty as if every drop of liquid in his body had been sponged up by the desert heat. But no one had thought to offer him any water.

A sudden gust of wind surprisingly slatted the canvas top of the truck. He heard someone shout, and a motor started up somewhere. There was very little he could see from under the canvas. The night had just fallen, he supposed,

and he wondered how he could have dozed off in such dis-
comfort. Long ago, however, he had learned to take advantage
of any respite and try to recoup his energies for what might
come.

By twisting to one side, he could see the dim desert
landscape under the strangely hazy moon. They were in an
area of twisted rock formations, with, here and there, long
tongues of sand sifting down from above. The wind blew
again, in a second sudden gust, and sand stung his face and
his eyes. He dropped back to the shelter of his other position
on the truck floor.

Now there were more shouts and Arab curses and the
whine of a motor again and the spinning of wheels. The
wind moaned, plucked at the truck canvas, died again. He
saw the light of the moon fade away as something obscured
the sky.

A sandstorm was coming.

He wished he knew what time it was. Someone had
stolen his watch. He wished he had a cigarette. And water. Or
something to eat.

He tried to estimate and analyze his situation, but there
were too many unknown factors to permit him a glimpse of
any developing pattern. He thought wryly of Amr's turning
on him, like a spiteful, petty child. He should have expected
it, should have believed in the man's threats to punish him
for what Amr considered to be insolence. Or perhaps Washington had committed the gravest error of all in assuming that
the prince's political attitudes would make him favorable to
the West. Obviously, Washington's information had been
all wrong. Amr was not so far gone in dissipation as the
world believed. That one glimpse he'd had of the prince's
face before he'd been knocked out told quite a different story.
Under the soft fat there was a core of irony and hard
strength that should have died out long ago in the man.

All this made matters quite different from the original
picture Durell had received from Haggarty. Washington was
due for an unpleasant surprise. The trouble was, Durell
thought, he should have spotted these underlying attitudes in
Bogo sooner than this, should have been forewarned and
taken the man's threats seriously. Now it might be that
he had brought back to Jidrat the one man who could really
take this tiny but important country out of the orbit of the
West.

When the storm came a few moments later, it struck like a hammer blow, with the howling of a thousand devils. A vast hissing roar blotted out all other sound. The truck trembled and shook under the impact of the wind. Sand flew in under the canvas of the truck and rippled in swift layers across the plank floor, stinging his eyes and his cheeks, crawling into his nostrils and his ears. He could not breathe. He lay on his side on the floor, doubled up, trying to mask his face with his arm to provide some kind of filter for his lungs. But his effort was only partially successful.

With the wind came a biting cold that set him to shivering. The shouts of the Al Murra were drowned in the tumult of the storm. No one came to the truck. He wondered if he had been abandoned by the others, who were better able to take shelter, or perhaps forgotten by those who had made him a prisoner.

He tried to loosen the thongs that held his wrists behind him. Not a chance. He rolled over, coughing. Sand gritted his eyes, and he squeezed them shut. The storm howled, the truck shook. The hissing blast of sand was scouring the paint off the metal body of the truck. He coughed again, felt sand creeping up over his legs, filling the truck. A feeling of panic touched him. He fought it. The very violence of the storm meant that it couldn't last too long. But it might go on long enough to bury him, in his helpless state, and slowly suffocate him.

He wondered where everyone else had gone.

He yelled once, and felt the sand slash into his open mouth and grate between his teeth, and he did not yell again. He wriggled to one side of the truck and tried to scrape the thongs against the metal hooks that held the canvas. Dimly, then, in a momentary lull, when the wind suddenly died, he heard shouting and confusion from Ibrahim's men.

Someone scratched at the back of the truck.

"Durell?"

He sat up, listening. There was more shouting from the distant head of the column and the grinding of a truck's motor trying to start. He could see nothing in the dark night. Then the back flap of the canvas was opened and someone moved inside, wearing a dark Arab robe. He smelled perfume.

"Zoraya, what—"

"Be still. I have a knife and a gun for you."

"But you can't—"

"I cannot let you stay like this either. They are planning to kill you. Don't you know that? Far inland, in the desert, when they feel safe and wish for some amusement. I heard them talking." She paused. Her face was dim as she knelt beside him inside the truck. "And a terrible thing has happened."

"What?"

"The Al Murra are no longer loyal to Amr. It was a trick. They belong to the Q'adi Ghezri's movement and Ibn Ibrahim expects a huge reward for killing both you and Amr."

"It didn't look that way on the beach."

"They were amusing themselves."

"How do you know all this?"

"Abdhuahram, the nakhoda, warned me. He is loyal to Amr."

"Good. We need him."

The girl leaned against him, her soft body trembling a little as she felt along his arms and wrists. A moment later there was a sharp jerk, and his wrists were free. Then his ankles. He knelt and massaged his wrists. A gun was thrust into his hands. He could see her face only as the faintest of ovals. Her hair brushed his cheek.

"And Amr?"

"Abdhuahram will carry him."

"Carry him?"

"They . . . they fell upon Amr all at once, as a great joke. It . . . it was terrible. He asked for food and they served him with such a show of deference, and all the time they were laughing and laughing because it was such a great joke to them. He did not know it. He could not guess how it was. When they were deliberately clumsy and spilled coffee, he jumped up and kicked the Arab who did it—thinking he was still held in high esteem, he was still Prince Amr al-Maari who commanded their loyalty. He flew into a rage and demanded punishment for the Arab who was so careless as to spill coffee on his royal personage."

The girl halted, then went on bitterly. "Ibn Ibrahim asked him what punishment he wanted them to give the Arab, and Amr insisted on twenty lashes. They then had the Arab plead for mercy, beg Amr to reduce the sentence, let him go free. Meanwhile, I could see there was something wrong—and so did Abdhuahram—because they were laugh-

ing and joking behind Amr's back. When Amr refused to ease
the punishment, Ibn Ibrahim suddenly threw Amr to the
ground and handed one of his men the whip. And the
sentence was carried out, not upon the slave but upon
Prince Amr himself."

Durell straightened. "Twenty lashes?" he whispered.

"Yes."

"And then?"

"He was given to me and Abdhuahram to care for, to keep
alive until they are ready for more amusements. But that is
not the worst of it for Amr. The worst is what happened to
his spirit when he saw he was no longer a 'prince' to the
Al Murra."

"I can imagine," Durell said gently.

"No. No, you cannot. It is impossible. He . . . he is like
one who has died inside. He says nothing. He looks at
nothing. He can only remember the humiliation, the way
the dirty, howling tribesmen played this trick upon his
dignity. Against this, the lashes of the whip were nothing."

"Where is Amr now?"

"Coming. Abdhuahram carries him. During this storm we
have our only chance to escape. We can use this truck."

The wind lifted again, buffeting the truck. Durell jumped
off the truck's tail gate and held up his arms and the girl
dropped with him to the flinty ground. He could see the dim
lights up ahead in Ibrahim's column. Then they ran around
to the cab of the truck. It was deserted by the driver, who
had evidently sought companionship with the others while
they waited out the storm. The windshield was covered with
sand. Durell brushed it off. He turned and saw the giant
nakhoda holding Prince Amr in his arms.

"Get in the cab," he ordered.

"Yes, effendi. You will drive?"

Durell looked at Zoraya, who nodded. "We can hide in
the ruins of Ain Gemilha," she said. "I know where we
are. It is only a few miles from here. But we must hurry!"

The nakhoda carried Amr around to the back of the
truck and Durell climbed up into the cab with Zoraya. He
thought he heard someone shout from far off, but the wind
was too strong and noisy and he could not be certain. Then
lights began flickering again from the head of the column,
as if men were running toward them. Durell stamped on the
starter, heard the motor whine and grind for what seemed an

eternity. It finally caught with a roar. He slammed the engine into gear and they lurched off to the right. He had to snap on the headlights. In the glare from the twin beams there was nothing to see but the wild, blinding turmoil of blowing sand driving straight at them. Nevertheless, it was better than total darkness.

"Go on," the girl said. "They will not follow yet. In a few minutes you will come to a road, and we can feel our way from there. I will guide you."

Durell tried to look back to see if they were being followed, but behind the truck he could see nothing but a blinding swirl of dark, wind-driven sand.

The truck faltered, coughed, stalled, jolted on again. They had to halt twice when the storm grew too violent. The wind was too strong for them to go around to the back and see how Amr and Abdhuahram were faring. The second time they stopped, Durell cut the headlights and sat in total darkness with the girl. Sand hissed along the metal sides of the truck, whispered through cracks around the doors and windows.

"It will soon be over," the girl said.

She sat close to him. It was cold in the desert now. The wind was a demon, howling for their lives, shaking the heavy truck, making the windows rattle. He felt her shiver.

"What will you do now?" she asked Durell.

"I don't know yet."

"You were so sure the Jidratti would follow Amr if you once brought him home. But you see what has happened."

"Was the Al Murra tribe always loyal to Amr's family?"

She was silent for a moment. "No. No, not always."

Something in her voice made him ask, "What is it, Zoraya? What are you thinking of?"

"I am reminded of the time I was kidnapped, on my wedding day. The day I married Amr I was so happy," she whispered. "I was only eight years old, you know, but one is trained for an early marriage and taught what to expect from life. And then, all in a moment, everything was changed and my life was destroyed, my future made homeless . . . and Amr no longer loved me."

"You were both children that day."

"A child in the desert cannot stay a child for many years. I knew all there was to know about my destiny and my future life—until the men came and there was all that shooting and one of them grabbed me and took me out here in the desert and held me for ransom. Ever since then, Amr refused to look upon me. He thinks I was defiled. But it is not true. It isn't true!" the girl whispered in anguish. "They did not touch me. Yet he would not listen. He still will not listen."

"Was it a tribal feud?" Durell asked.

"Yes. The Al Murra and the al-Maari family were enemies for a long time. When I was returned, Ibn Ibrahim swore allegiance to Amr. But you see what such an oath is worth today."

Durell sat up straighter. "It was the Al Murra who kidnapped you on your wedding day?"

"Yes. Why?"

"Then they . . . it's not a fair test," he said tightly. "It doesn't mean that the people of Jidrat will reject Amr."

She was silent a long time. Durell felt her shivering in the cold fingers of the sandy wind that gripped the vehicle.

"What will happen to you, Durell, if you fail?" she whispered. "How you must hate Amr for turning on you as he did! It was such a petty, foolish thing to do. To hate you for trying to help him. It made me ill; I wanted to weep, to strike at him. When I saw you lying there with that Al Murra ready to kill you—and Amr watching it all and wanting it to happen to you simply because you risked your life to help him come home where he belongs—"

"I was only doing my job."

"It was more than just the job," she said. "More than that. You hide behind your duty as I've hidden behind false hopes. Neither of us are true to ourselves. I have lived in a dream world all my life—since my wedding day. And you . . . you are good and kind and strong and you do things in the name of duty which you do not really have to do."

He said nothing.

"We will not live to see the sunset tomorrow," the girl whispered. "It is hopeless, what you've tried to do."

"No."

"If Amr were a man, if he had any strength—"

"I haven't given up on him yet."

He felt her turn on the rough seat. She sat very close to him.

"Put your arm around me," she said. "I'm so cold."

He held her gently. She was shivering. She twisted con-

vulsively and lifted her face to his, and he kissed her. Her lips
were cold and tremulous at first. She spoke against his lips.
"I don't want to talk about dying tomorrow. I'm sorry. I
know it will happen, but now I feel as if there were no one
else alive in the world except you and me—here, in this little
box of darkness in the middle of the wind and the sand. . . ."

"Zoraya—"

"No, let me dream a little longer. It will end soon enough.
I have been dreaming all my life, it seems. If I were a wiser
woman, I would have forced myself to see what Amr was,
long ago. I would have faced the truth of what was in my
heart."

"We won't die tomorrow," Durell said. But he did not
believe it.

"There will be no escape. Please. Tell me something,"
she whispered. "Tell me the truth at this moment. Did you
really never forget me? In all the years between then and
now, did you still think of me and remember that morning
you took Amr to see me, down on the Chesapeake?"

"Yes," he admitted. "I never forgot you."

"I fell in love with you," she whispered. "I think perhaps
I have loved you ever since. Is that so foolish?"

"You were only twelve. . . ."

"Yes. Only twelve," she said bitterly.

He felt a vast well of sorrow deepening inside him. He
held her closer. There was no way to bridge the worlds that
lay between them. In Zoraya there was a deep and terrible
struggle between the blood of her English ancestors and the
blood of her Arab parents; between everything she had been
trained to be, all she had been taught to submit to, and the
Western world that she had lived in, in exile, for so long.
There were the years between them, too. He did not know
what to say to her that might comfort her. Words were nothing—like the gusts of wind that threw the sands of the desert
around the truck and buried them in the howling darkness,
making the silence inside the cab all the more intense and
pitiful.

He kissed her again, and this time her lips were quick and
warm and demanding. He felt her whole being pressing
against him, wanting him, like a cry of despair against the
inevitable fate she knew waited for them when the dawn
came.

Perhaps she was right, he thought. Long ago he had taught

Amr to weigh and calculate the odds of a gambling throw.
The wise gambler knew how to call a halt and cut his losses
when his hand was too weak to win. All he had here with
him now was Amr, and Amr was too weak, too crushed by
what had happened to him when the Al Murra lashed him
like a common slave back there in the desert camp. How
could he hope to have this man stand up tomorrow against
the wild mobs of revolution in Jidrat? It was too much to ask.
He had no idea of what the situation in the city might be
or of how he could use Amr when the dawn came.

Yes, they might all die tomorrow.

He held the girl closer and felt the warm wetness of her
tears on the cheek against his face.

The wind blew and the sand hissed against the windows
and the night closed in around them.

Chapter Fifteen

THE WIND reached out from the desert and blew clouds of turbulent sand out to the sea and screamed over the city of Jidrat. At ten o'clock in the morning all fighting had stopped, all living creatures had sought shelter from the biting, stinging elements. The wind found the open corners of Faiz and came tumbling into the palace, blowing draperies and tapestries, overturning light furniture and screens, whistling through windows and spreading sand everywhere on the polished tile floors.

The Imam Yazid could not sleep. Sleep came with difficulty to an old man of his years, he thought, and tonight, besides, had been different from all the other nights of his life. He had seen wars and desert campaigns when the Englisi had first come and the tribes had carried on guerilla warfare for years.

He'd been ambitious then. The al-Maaris were an old family, the rightful rulers of Jidrat. He'd been young and strong in the battles he'd fought before he won his way to Faiz, the seat of government.

His mind turned and twisted as he lay on his couch and listened to the desert wind. He was old and tired now. He remembered his strength against the Englisi. When had this weakness begun? Perhaps when Amr's father was killed in a minor tribal skirmish and Amr himself, his hope for the future, changed, and left Jidrat and refused to return.

The old man sighed. The sound was faint against the clamor of the wind. He remembered the wedding of Amr and Zoraya and the treachery of the Al Murra, who kidnapped the child bride. Amr had changed then. The hope that Amr would come home and rule with kindness and intelligence was long given up.

Yazid's mind drifted back through history to the Portuguese who came to Arabia in the fourteenth century and stayed for almost two hundred years. They were followed by internecine warfare between the Sunnite and Shiite sects of Islam and by the rise of the early Wahabis and of Ibn Saud who only cast a patina of modernity over his people.

133

Someday, Yazid prayed, the Mahdi would come and all would be well in Islam. But not the Q'adi Ghezri, that pretentious vulture in his black robe, stirring up the people as he rode about on his white donkey and pretended poverty while he lived with luxurious riches. . . .

The old man sighed and went to the balcony to look out over the stormy city in the night. He ignored the cold wind, the bite of the driven sand. His books were behind him. Useless to read, he thought, while the mob rioted and the guards repulsed the first outrageous attack against Faiz. He found no consolation in the philosophy of Al Gazel or Kindi; nothing to help him in the historic works of the sages Ibn Batuta and Masudi. The heavy leather books gave him no answers. He had tried to read the formal, exaggerated style of the court poets of the eighth century who had flourished during the Baghdad caliphate—Abu al-Atahiya and Abu Nuwais. Their measured cadences sounded hollow under the thud of mortars and the billowing smoke that moved over the city.

Too late. . . . Tomorrow, at dawn, the end would come.

The old man was not afraid of the dark city or the next hours. An old man knows no fears except those that always live within him. His heartbeat was erratic, his breath labored, and the strength was gone from his limbs.

He had made mistakes. He knew the inflamed mob did not understand the slogans they chanted. They lived in poverty and hunger and filth. He had taken the West's oil money and built schools and hospitals and tried to see that no man suffered from extreme want.

But it had not been enough.

The world moved too swiftly for his people to catch up. But that must not be. There was an answer somewhere. Not from the Soviets, with their patient, guileful promises, waiting the way a tiger waits to spring upon his prey. Not from the West, either, the old man thought. His mind moved clearly toward the ultimate question.

The Jidratti had to find the future in themselves. It would be a slow and painful process. To hope that one leap, by fire and destruction, could bring equality was an impossible dream. More education was needed, and a dignity that could come only with time and new generations.

Meanwhile, there was the dawn.

He would try to hold back the mob, but his troops were

exhausted, sick with firing on their own people. In the morning the gate would be breached and the mob would howl for plunder in old Faiz. He looked down at the distant wall, in darkness now. From the main gate a wide avenue swept uphill to the palace; a boulevard lined with palms and gardens, an oasis of green in the limestone hills.

He could see the dirty, panting mob, shrieking their hate.

He would meet them at the Bab es-Salam, the Gate of Peace. Yes, there, just inside the gate. He would stand alone and tell them the truth. They were his children—all of them. They would obey.

They would see their Imam stand before them and they would stop and listen and he would speak to them, and it would be ended.

There was nothing else he could do.

Thinking this, listening to the wind that screamed around the sprawling palace, he felt the bite of the cold night air at last, and he went slowly back into his chamber. He did not sleep. From his bedside he took his Koran and slowly began to read.

The wind seemed to sweep the holy words through his mind, tumbling them away into darkness. . . .

In the Hotel al-Zaysir, in the cup of the darkened city, Naomi Haledi lay staring into the dark night. She had been awake for hours. She was hungry and thirsty but she was afraid to leave the hotel room that Esme Kenton had spirited her into.

Why had she slept so long? She remembered that the Englishwoman had given her a mild sedative and urged her to rest. In her state of exhaustion, the pill had worked like a blow on the head. But now she was awake again, staring—wide-eyed—at the high, dark ceiling, and she could not understand how she had been able to forget her danger.

Where was Mrs. Kenton? There was no note, no word at all. No one had come to the room since she had wakened herself, and she heard nothing at all inside the rambling corridors of the hotel.

If Esme did not come back, what could she do? She was trapped here. It would be easy enough for Ta'arife's secret police to find her, even with all the confused fighting in Jidrat.

It was hopeless to think of escape. And useless to hope.

Yet she felt no fear now. Her heart beat calmly in her breast. How many times had she waited like this for Kolia, in their secret apartment in Budapest? Like clandestine lovers, even though she wore his wedding ring. It was over. All over.

And she no longer thought of Kolia Mikelnikov as a monster that had killed her gentle father in the square that day. She listened to the wild wind over the city and felt a new understanding. They were all trapped—all of them—living as best they could. Her first hatred toward Kolia had been useful, sustaining her in her flight through strange lands until she had come home to Israel.

Home, she thought. Yes, it was home. Where there was new strength and a pioneer spirit that seized the desert and changed it, with patience and love, and made it bloom again as the Bible said it had in the old days.

She no longer hated Kolia. She could remember only their love.

Tomorrow, she thought as she listened to the wind, it would end, and she decided to remember Kolia only as her husband, as her gentle lover. It would be better if things ended like that.

In the hotel room directly below, never suspecting how near she was, Major Kolia Mikelnikov lay fully dressed on his bed and also thought of Budapest and of the past and of the future.

He listened to the wind, and although this was a desert wind, full of stinging sand that whipped the city, he remembered the snowy plains before Moscow when the Nazis advanced and he thought of the fighting that last frozen winter in the brittle reeds along the river bank.

It all seemed long ago in the past. Yet it was part of today, too. He thought of all the killing, and the war that had not ended yet for him, and he remembered the men he had known who were now only skeletons in their graves. All gone, gone.

Like Naomi had gone, leaving him desolate and alone.

Then he thought of what had to be done tomorrow, when the storm ended. Somehow, he had to find Durell, the American agent, in all this alien confusion. Somehow, he had to kill him.

Kill or be killed. That was the rule, the law of those who always lived with death.

He touched the cold barrel of his Tokarev, beside him. The gun was ready. Waiting. He would do it himself, trusting no one else.

Otherwise he could never go home. His superiors would condemn him. And life beat too strongly in him to surrender now.

He did not know yet how to accomplish his mission. But it would be done. He felt sure of his strength and ability.

He listened to the wind and he remembered rain in the streets of Budapest and the orders General Murov had given him. He had protested, but Murov had not listened. Murov had sneered at his protest against shooting down innocent people in the old squares and streets of the beautiful city on the Danube. His words had been met with cold suspicion.

"I know about your lady love," Murov had said. "The little Jewess, eh? The pretty little actress you've been seeing."

"Comrade General, I can't say—"

"A bit of fun is all right. A man must relax. And you have no wife and family back home. You were very young during the war. One would think . . . but no one blames you, Kolia, though you could have chosen a woman more wisely."

He had wanted to tell Murov he was married to Naomi. But then all would be ruined. It was not the moment—with rebellion in the streets, with revolution rising through all the Hungarian countryside. It was incredible how those people had fought: with sticks and stones, young boys streaking from doorways to climb up on passing tanks and drop homemade grenades down the turret on the crew. It was incredible.

How they hated us! Kolia thought. Why?

He knew why, now. Since Budapest, he had been trusted with missions in the West. He had read the free press of the world and now he understood what he had done.

It was all wrong. But he did not know the final answer. It was neither all black nor all white. You did what you were told, however, or you were lost. They killed you, otherwise. One way or another, you lost if you tried to break free of life's traps.

He thought of his meeting with Durell in Geneva, three days ago. He was like Durell in so many ways, he thought.

He tried to think of how it would be when he killed him. He would just do it, he decided. And then it would be over.

The soldiers drowsed, sprawling, in the lobby of the Hotel al-Zaysir. They were restless, troubled by the wind. The foreign guests in their rooms offered no trouble. Only a madman would try to escape the security of the al-Zaysir. If they went into the city, they would be torn apart by the mobs. No, there was nothing to worry about here.

A dim light shone in the bar and T. P. Fenner, the American consul, helped himself to a new bottle of bourbon from the shelves, wondering where Messaoud had gone in the day's confusion. Fenner worried about the state of the consulate building, but Ta'arife had assured him there would be no more wanton destruction of property. Tomorrow there would be a last assault on Faiz, and then law and order would be restored.

Fenner felt badly shaken by the violent disorder. The looting and burning and deliberately ineffective police, who grinned while shops were smashed and people were killed— all this, and the pall of smoke like a shroud over the city— well, it shook a man up; gave him a feeling of unreality that he could escape only by seeking sanity for himself in bourbon.

He knew he had failed in his job.

He could go back to his own quarters, he supposed, but he preferred the al-Zaysir, not trusting his Arab servants now. He certainly did not want to be alone, because then the wind would snatch him up and strip his flesh to the bone and show him naked, as he really was.

He was badly frightened.

The bottle of bourbon didn't help either. He had had so much that under ordinary circumstances he'd have gone out like a light—stinko, blotto. But this time the bourbon only made him feel colder and more alone.

He felt as if he had made a whole series of mistakes somewhere in the recent past. But he couldn't figure out what they were. He'd done his job, hadn't he? Fulfilled all the duties and obligations of a U.S. Consul, right? Was it his fault if these crazy people didn't respect the United States, if they shrieked, "Kill the Englisi!" and then, in the same breath, screamed, "Kill the Americani!"?

He had never suspected the depth and violence of the searing hatred that engulfed the city now.

And he felt as if it were all directed against him. Against T. P. Fenner personally—his own body, his own identity.

They'd like to tear him apart. He was the object of their hatred.

And he could not understand why.

He drank again, deeply, from the bottle he'd helped himself to behind the al-Zaysir bar. There was no servant in sight. They were all gone, merged into the howling mob. He drank again and wiped his mouth and sighed. His heart pounded strangely. He felt cold. The quiet of the city was misleading. Two o'clock in the morning, and the windstorm had swept the revolution right off the streets. He wished it would keep blowing forever. But he did not delude himself. He knew that at dawn, when the storm was over, all red hell would break loose again.

"Mr. Fenner?"

He turned violently, clutching the bottle, his round face reflecting fear. Then he saw that it was Colonel Ta'arife. The colonel looked tired. His sharp, dark, ambitious face was worn by the failure of his coup to achieve an immediate success yesterday.

"Mr. Fenner? I want a word with you."

"Sure. Of course, Colonel."

"Are you feeling well, Mr. Fenner? You look ill."

"No, I'm fine. Just fine. It's fine here," Fenner said.

"Yes. Well, what I wanted to speak to you about was this Captain MacPherson who came to your office to see you yesterday."

"Who?"

"MacPherson," Ta'arife said patiently. "From the *Atlantic Maid*."

"Oh, him. I couldn't help him. I'm afraid he didn't get much satisfaction from me, Colonel."

"I know this. But he asked you to give sanctuary to the Israeli woman who was a passenger on his ship, did he not?"

"Sure, but I couldn't do a thing like that," Fenner said. He wanted to please Ta'arife. The man didn't look right. There was a funny look on his face. You couldn't trust these people, Fenner thought. Stick a knife in your back while they smile at you. He said, "It wasn't anything the Consulate could or ought to do, you see."

"Yes. What did Captain MacPherson do then?"

"Do? I don't know."

"Of course you know," Ta'arife said patiently. He spoke like a cop who knew his business. Cops were cops everywhere, Fenner thought; but this one couldn't keep order in his own town. Hell, no. Then he heard Ta'arife say, "You sent MacPherson to try to get help for the Israeli girl elsewhere, did you not? You wanted to help this spy, did you not?"

"Oh, come now, I don't know that she's a spy—a young woman like that. . . ."

"My business is intelligence, Mr. Fenner. Of course she is a spy. You know that too. I know the ship did not just happen to break down and make port in Jidrat at just this time by coincidence, by simple chance. Did you know that she isn't on the ship now?"

"No, I didn't. Where is she?"

"That is what you must find out for me."

"Me? How can I find out?"

"You must think. You must help me. Where did MacPherson go after he left your office? You gave him a suggestion, did you not?"

"I . . . I mentioned Mrs. Kenton. . . ." Fenner faltered.

"Ah."

"Really now, this girl can't be as dangerous as all that."

"You know nothing about it, if you will pardon my saying so, Mr. Fenner. I say she is dangerous. I say we must find her at once. So MacPherson went to Esme Kenton?"

"Yes."

"And she went to the ship for the girl?"

"I don't know."

"And then she took the girl ashore, is that not right?"

Fenner's mouth and throat felt dry. He reached for the bourbon bottle, saw Ta'arife's dark eyes follow his hand, and he suddenly pulled back his fingers, feeling strangely ashamed. Goddam it, he thought. What's the matter with me? His stomach burned and churned and his heart lurched when Ta'arife smiled at him.

"Colonel, you could help me, too, you know. I've got to get a cable off to my government. They want to know—"

"All communication except through Radio Jidrat is forbidden."

"Yes. Well, I thought just a message—"

"When matters are settled here. When security and law and order are established again. Tomorrow, Mr. Fenner. I simply want to be sure that it was Mrs. Esme Kenton you sent the captain to see. That explains a great deal of it."

"Does it?" Fenner asked.

"Where is Mrs. Kenton now? Do you know?"

"Why, in her room, I suppose."

"Did you see her arrive here at the al-Zaysir?"

"Why, yes, I—"

Ta'arife waited.

Fenner said nothing. His face felt hot.

"Well?" Ta'arife said. He breathed softly. "Was she alone, Mr. Fenner?"

"I don't know."

"You saw her with your own eyes."

"Yeah. Yes."

"The girl was with her?"

"I didn't really get a good look," Fenner mumbled. "I didn't think anything at all about it."

"Was the girl with Mrs. Kenton?"

"A girl was with her. I don't know who she was."

"I see. Thank you."

Fenner watched the slim, elegantly uniformed Arab turn and walk out of the bar. Ta'arife walked straighter, more confidently than when he'd come in. What in hell? Fenner thought vaguely. What did I tell him? Nothing. Maybe the girl *is* a spy. Anyway, it was nothing to him. Nothing at all.

Ta'arife was gone. Fenner reached for the bourbon and splashed a drink in his glass. He held the glass in both hands because he was shaky and felt sick to his stomach.

He wished the damned wind would stop blowing now.

Chapter Sixteen

THE STORM ended an hour before dawn, blowing itself out over the Arabian Sea: a high cloud of churning sand spinning away into the darkness. The stars came out. The air was still and cold. The moon shone on the smoothly rippled sand, the dark cliffs, the jagged flint plateaus, the black and ominous ridges of the *djebels* in the interior.

Durell heaved against the door of the truck cab. The sand had blown up in a long smooth dune against it, overlapping the front wheels and the motor hood. It took a few moments of hard effort to shove the door open wide enough so he could slip out. Zoraya followed him. Her face was calm. There was no trace of the tears he had seen her shed.

"Do you know where we are?" he asked her.

"Near Ain Gemilha. I can tell by the shape of that ridge," she said, pointing.

He looked back, over the way they had come. There was no trace of their tire tracks in the smooth tongues of sand that shone white in the moonlight.

"What about the Al Murra?"

"They will not follow us out."

"You seem sure of that."

"They will think we are dead. Buried by the storm."

He walked around to the back of the truck, slogging through the soft, yielding sand that had blown here, too, under body and between the wheels. He wondered if they were stuck here, if they could get the motor started, but he decided to put that off for now.

"Effendi?"

He saw the nakhoda, Abdhuahram, jump from the tail gate under the canvas that was weighted with sand. The nakhoda looked barbaric with his thick black beard, his turban, his naked torso.

"Effendi, you are both safe?"

"Yes," Durell said. "And the prince?"

Tha nakhoda shrugged. "I did what I could for him. His back was bleeding where Ibrahim lashed him. He is ill."

"Ill? How do you mean?"

The big man shrugged again. "He will not speak to me."

"Why not?"

"See for yourself, effendi."

Durell lifted the canvas flap. Moonlight flooded the sheltered body of the truck. Amr al-Maari sat cross-legged on the floor, his hands on his knees, his eyes staring at nothing at all. For a moment, Durell could not even tell if the small man was breathing. He saw that the past twenty-four hours had squeezed weight and fat off the man; Amr's face looked thinner, with a trace of the sharp fox features Durell remembered from long ago.

"Bogo," he said. "What is it?"

Amr did not move.

"Are you sick?" Durell asked.

"Yes," Amr whispered.

"Where? What is it? We'll get a doctor today—"

"It is in my heart. You can do nothing for me. I am going to die today."

"Nonsense. Today you are going into Jidrat with me and make everything right again."

Amr did not move or reply.

"Did you hear me, Bogo?"

"I heard you. I was whipped like a slave, and they laughed like jackals at Prince Amr al-Maari. They played with me, made sport of me, and I was a fool." Amr sighed.

"We all make mistakes."

"My whole life has been a mistake."

"That's as Allah wills."

"I am not a true believer. There is no consolation for me there."

Durell said, "Are you hungry? Thirsty?"

"No. Do not trouble yourself with me, Cajun."

"Are you still my enemy? Or my friend?"

Amr did not answer.

Durell tried to start the truck. It would not start. The motor ground fitfully for a few moments, and then the battery was dead and nothing happened. He felt the emptiness of the desert holding them in a giant cold hand. When the sun came up, that would end. It would be hot. And the sun would kill them if they remained here.

"How far are we from Jidrat?" he asked.

Zoraya answered. "A few miles. Six or seven."

"Can we walk?"

"For a little time. But not in the heat of the day."

"We have to walk," Durell said.

"I will try," she said. "But Amr will not come with us."

"We'll see about that," Durell told her.

He went to the back of the truck. The nakhoda sat on the sand there. Durell looked inside and saw that Amr had not moved. He still stared sightlessly at the shame of his lashing.

"Come on, Bogo. We've got to walk."

"To Jidrat?"

"Yes. To your grandfather, the Imam."

"And when we get there?"

"You will do what must be done. Come down out of the truck now."

"I would rather die here."

"But I don't want to die," Durell said. "And neither does Zoraya. Would you want her to die here like this, alone in the desert with no chance to get help?"

Amr turned his head slightly and stared at Durell for a long time out of expressionless eyes. "She loves you," he whispered.

"No."

"She loves you. She is not mine now."

"She has always been yours. Always. Before your wedding as children, and afterward. After the Al Murra took her, she was still yours. Why don't you believe her?"

"Did she tell you this?"

"And more."

"I wish . . . I would like to know the truth—and believe —"

"Ask her again. You're not too proud now. Your pride has been humbled, Bogo. Maybe that's a good thing. Maybe now you know what it is to be a human being, an ordinary mortal."

"Yes. I know pain. And humiliation. And sorrow."

"And fear?"

"No."

"Love?"

"I have always loved her," Amr said quietly.

He climbed down out of the truck.

As he did so, the ground leaped with the explosion.

The high scarp of limestone cliff stood clear and sharp,

about a quarter of a mile away, seen through the desert night under the waning moonlight. The cliff dissolved in the explosion.

Durell, who had been standing to face that way, saw the first streak of flame, the burst of white concussive force.

He did not know where it came from or what caused it.

The solid rock of the earth seemed to leap skyward, all in one movement, almost all in one piece. The sheet of flame spread. There were minor explosions, like a sub-harmony in some madman's symphony. The cliff leaped up and seemed to hang there against the face of the moon, and then it crumbled, broke apart and cracked into vast fragments that also seemed to hang against the sky before slowly falling with a vast, rolling thunder of sound that struck them like the force of a giant's blow.

Wind and sand came first, and then sound—crushing them with the impact, driving them to the earth with the surprising blast. There seemed to be no end to it. Explosion after explosion rocked the desert and the night. Stones fell all around them, clattering on the flint, thudding into the sand.

Durell shouted soundlessly into the blast and threw Zoraya under the shelter of the truck and then pulled Amr with him.

The nakhoda was not so fortunate.

A stone the size of a melon, jagged on one side, came arching invisibly from the broken cliff along with all the other stones, and it struck Abdhuahram in the back of the head. For one moment, he was aware of the sound of the earth's being torn apart, and for another moment he knew an anguished pain, and then he toppled forward and slid down the sand back toward the truck, his giant's body asprawl. He was already dead.

Durell, hugging the earth, waited for the sounds to die. The whole thing did not last long, although at the time it seemed to take an eternity.

When silence returned, deep and awesome, he looked at Zoraya.

"Are you all right?"

"Yes. But what—"

"It was a storage dump for ammunition and supplies. Nothing else could have done that."

"In the cliff?"

"There are probably caves there," he said. He looked at Amr. "And you? You're not hurt?"

Amr was staring off into the desert. "Someone is coming," he said. "It is a woman."

Esme Kenton had remembered the gun, finally, after a long time. She did not know how much time went by before she thought of it. And even then—when she found herself looking at the small, pearl-handled .28, the ridiculous little mechanism that Paul had given her so long ago—it had no meaning for her.

It lay under the table in the cave where Messaoud had kicked it when she had failed to save Paul's life.

She felt cold. Cold. The fat Arab with the huge paunch had finally let her alone. He sat near the mouth of the cave, looking out at the storm. She heard the wind for a long time without knowing what it was. She thought the sound of the storm and the sand was something inside her head because she ached all over, deep inside her body; because they had been cruel and brutal and deliberately tortuous to her. Messaoud had dragged her partly to one side after the fat one was through—Messaoud, gasping and panting, with his bloody eye still dripping. Messaoud, however, had fainted, lying across her.

She could feel his thin, bony weight across her stomach now. He had been quiet for a long time. The fat Arab sat at the mouth of the cave and talked to himself, but his voice was scarcely audible above the roaring tumult of the sandstorm outside.

She waited for a long time.

Once, she turned her head and looked at Paul's body. Then she turned her head away and did not look at him again.

The storm had just ended when she realized she was looking at the forgotten gun.

It was loaded. It was about four feet away.

It could have been a million miles away because Messaoud still lay, sprawled out upon her, unconscious. He had stopped bleeding but she could feel where his blood had dried upon her naked leg. He was groaning softly with each breath he took. A sound that went, "Agh-sgh-uh," with a regular, hypnotic rhythm. The other Arab paid no attention to him, or to her now. He was only interested in the storm.

She moved her left arm, the hand that was nearest the table. Just a little bit. An inch, and then another inch. Messaoud went on groaning. She tried not to move any other part of her body, not to awaken him. She knew that when he woke up and found himself blind in one eye—when it all came back to him—well, then he would kill her.

So she had to kill him first.

She felt very calm. She felt detached from the pain that lay in her body. She felt as if her hand had a life of its own, creeping toward the gun that lay in the shadows under the table.

The gasoline lantern on top of the table sputtered and she thought it was going to go out; but then the hissing flame steadied and went on shining, with its garish brightness, on the inside of the cave.

She got her arm stretched out straight away from her toward the table, as far as she could go, and then she tried to stretch her wrist and her fingers.

The gun was too far away. She couldn't reach it.

Messaoud groaned and moved. She lifted her hips as he shifted his weight, and she slid a few inches closer to the table.

Not enough. She tried again.

Messaoud rolled over her and his head fell from her hip and he hit the hard floor of the cave and became conscious again with a loud groan. He raised his head and looked at her and she saw the clotted horror of his torn eye and she saw the way his other eye looked at her and then she lurched up and grabbed the gun and caught it up in her hand.

Messaoud shrieked a warning and then she rolled away and held up the gun and fired it. She saw the bullet go into his face, a small black hole dotting his hollow cheek like magic. She fired again, and then again, and Messaoud fell away from her and his body twitched. But she didn't go near him again.

The fat Arab was on his feet in the mouth of the cave, staring stupidly at her.

There were six bullets in the .28. She had used three on Messaoud. She spent two on the fat man, feeling very cold and sober as she shot him once in the stomach and once in the head. She knew the fat one was dead before he fell.

Messaoud was groaning, flapping his arms, rolling around.

Esme stood up slowly. She felt very strong and clear-headed. She walked across the cave to where Messaoud lay groaning and knelt beside him with the gun in her hand.

"Messaoud, can you hear me?"

"Yes, Englisi lady. Help me, Englisi lady."

"All right, Messaoud."

She put the gun to his ear and squeezed the trigger and sent the last bullet crashing into Messaoud's brain.

She did not consider it an act of mercy.

Now she felt very steady. She knew exactly what she had to do. She picked up her torn clothes and put them on quickly but carefully. She stared at the cave opening. Yes, the wind had died. The storm was over. She looked back only once, before she left the cave.

"Good-bye, Paul, darling," she said.

Then she went out.

Paul had not told her where the arms cache was, but she knew. He didn't have to tell her. It could only be in one place—where he had been digging; in a new fissure he had mentioned last week and then never discussed again. When she had gone looking for it, alone, she had seen it was blocked up with stones. It was not far from the well of Ain Gemilha.

That was where Paul had found the arms.

She climbed down the path from the cliff to the narrow wadi where the Ford pickup truck was parked. She was surprised to see it still there, although there was no reason why it shouldn't have been. Still, it seemed as if it must have been someone else who drove out here with Messaoud so long ago, in the beginning of this night. Not Esme Kenton.

It did not take long to do what she had decided upon.

The wadi had sheltered the truck from the blowing sand. She had no trouble starting it. She saw by the position of the waning moon that it would soon be dawn. But that didn't matter. She backed out of the wadi and drove on down the road and in a very few minutes she was at the well of Ain Gemilha. There was a flashlight under the seat in the driver's cab. She took it out and went down the old, worn, circular stone stairway to the bottom of the cistern, where the sky was only a dim starlit circle above her.

She went to work on the stones which Paul had used to block up the fissure. Her fingernails broke and bled, but she didn't feel it.

The opening beyond was a tunnel that had been cut two thousand years ago by the pre-Nabateans who had built the walled town of Ain Gemilha. It was a common and wise practice in those ancient days to make sure of access to a water supply during times of war, when the town might be beseiged.

The arms were stacked in here, in the tunnel that led to the top of the ancient mound. Her flashlight touched stacks of boxes of ammunition, grenades, mortar shells, cannon shells, dynamite, rifles, machine guns, cartridge belts. Enough there to make sure the Q'adi could surprise his ally, Colonel Ta'arife, when the time was right for beginning his jihad against all the world.

"Well, Esme," she said aloud.

She laughed softly and forced open one of the wooden crates with a stone. It held grenades. She took one of the grenades and examined it carefully and saw that it was all right. Paul had once taken the trouble to show her such things when they found an abandoned arms dump in the Sahara desert, after the war.

None of it took very long.

She went down the tunnel to the entrance at the bottom of the cistern and there she pulled the pin from the grenade and threw it into the tunnel. Then she lay down flat on the hard, cold floor of the dry well.

When the explosions were over and the earth stopped shaking and the stones stopped falling, she got up and climbed up the steps again.

The Ford was wrecked. It could not be used. It did not seem to matter, however, and she started to walk along the road and presently she saw the truck and the two men— Durell and Amr—and the girl.

The first pearly light of dawn touched the eastern sky as Esme Kenton walked up to them and told them what had happened and what she had done.

Chapter Seventeen

COLONEL TA'ARIFE finished talking to his aides just as the first light touched the smoldering city. He met them in the Café Ozmani, and the aides were not military officers who had joined in the revolt that so far, with Faiz still standing, seemed to be a failure. These men were an evil-looking crew, scoured from the slums of the city. They were professional street agitators, orators, rabble rousers who knew how to inflame a crowd with well-chosen slogans about imperialism, oppression, and exploitation.

They listened and nodded their heads. Two of them yawned and grunted; they'd had a hard day yesterday. He told them they would die if they failed in this job. Many years ago, when Ta'arife went to Oxford in England, he was invited to partake of a typical English weekend that had included a fox hunt. He wished he could explain to these evil-looking men what a fox hunt implied; how the quarry was chivvied from covert to covert, driven and herded into position the way a sheepdog runs his herd of sheep. There was no way to explain all this. But he did the best he could.

His men understood. They said they would be ready.

Then he walked back through the empty streets that still had not wakened to the renewed growl of the mob that slept, spent from yesterday's exertions. It would begin soon. The animal would arise, the sleeping troops would yawn and scratch and drink their black coffee and look up at the loom of Faiz, above Jidrat, and they would wonder if today Allah would gather them all to his bosom in paradise.

He walked back to the Hotel al-Zaysir feeling a renewed confidence. The only thing missing, of course, was a report from Messaoud. But he was sure that Messaoud would learn from the Englishman, through his wife, where the Q'adi's arms were hidden. After that, the future would be clear.

It was plain that unless something extraordinary happened, something to whip the mob to a new frenzy, Faiz would continue to stand against him.

But the extraordinary thing was ready, at hand. And his six men were already gathering the material for Ta'arife's fox hunt.

He went into the Al-Zaysir, noting the sleepy, spitting platoon of soldiers who guarded the foreigners here, and went up to the second floor and knocked on Naomi Haledi's door.

She was sitting on the edge of the bed at the open window. The morning light was still dim and the cool air was deceptive. Soon the crushing heat of Arabia would return and smother all breath, inflame the lungs and the mind and the heart with insane passions. When the knock came, she stood up slowly, her hand at her throat.

"Esme?" she whispered.

The knock was repeated and the lever handle on the door went down, then up, then down again. "Who is it?" she called.

"Let me in, Miss Haledi." The answer came in English. "It is useless to resist. I am a friend. Believe me," Ta'arife said persuasively, "I am a friend. I have come here to help you."

She went to the door and unlocked it.

When she saw Ta'arife, she knew at once who he was. But she did not understand the compassionate smile on his full lips or the way he said gently, "Please do not be alarmed. I am your friend."

"My friend? I have no—"

"You should have remained on the ship," Ta'arife said. "It would have been less dangerous for you."

"You . . . you're concerned about my danger?"

"It would take too long to explain," Ta'arife said. "You understand the situation here. There must be no distractions. The people must not be diverted by discovering that you are in Jidrat."

"I meant no harm. I mean, I'm not a spy, you know."

"Of course I know that."

She stared incredulously at the slim, elegant Arab. Ta'arife's smile showed fine white teeth. She said, "Is this some kind of trick?" She found it difficult to breathe. She felt trapped. For her, the worst had happened, and so easily, so casually that she still could not believe that she had been caught in this room like this. "Is it?"

"Why must you believe we are all evil, all thirsting for

your blood? You are only a woman, after all. We see no danger in your presence here. But the street crowds might think . . ." He shrugged. "That is why I have come alone. You can see for yourself I have no one with me."

"Am I under arrest?"

"No."

"I don't understand why—"

"It is not difficult. I want you back on the ship, out of the way, so there will be no disturbance."

"I. . . I don't know what to say," she whispered.

"Come with me," he said.

"Where?"

"You must not be seen by the soldiers in the lobby. I have a car in back of the hotel. We can go that way."

She felt weak with relief. For a moment she was still confused, not daring to believe that this polite man was the ogre she had hidden from in such terror. She looked around the room. "I should leave a note for Esme Kenton."

"I will explain everything to her."

Ta'arife's eyes were very bright and amused. She could not understand his smile. She said, "You know, I am *not* a spy."

"That sort of thing is simple propaganda for the people. It is unfortunate, but that is the way of the world we live in. I am at heart a peaceful man. As an individual, I could be friends with anyone. Do you understand?" He shrugged expressively. "But as a soldier and as head of the national police, one has official duties. When I can be, I am lenient. As I am now. But you must hurry, please."

"Yes, of course."

"Do you want to take anything with you?"

She picked up her handbag. Its weight reminded her that she had the Luger. She held it casually. "Only this."

"Good. Let us go."

She followed him into the empty corridor and down the back service stairs and through the rear hall to the kitchen of the Hotel al-Zaysir. She did not know it was the same route Esme Kenton had taken many hours ago.

The kitchen was deserted. There would be no help today. She hurried through, following the colonel's slim, striding figure. She thought, joyously: It's almost too good to be true. I can hardly believe it. I'm safe. Nothing is going to happen to me after all. I was worried about nothing. Nothing at all.

Daylight had come. The alley behind the al-Zaysir—with

its steps going up under the archway and the native houses crowding close, balconies almost touching overhead—was still in cool shadow, however.

She followed Ta'arife up the steps under the archway.

At the head of the stone stairway in the alley stood four or five men.

They looked ominous in their ragged white robes. They were armed with a variety of weapons. They blocked the way at the head of the stairway under the arch and looked at her, staring.

Ta'arife halted. He smiled. "Wait," he said.

Naomi paused, expecting Ta'arife to order the men aside. Nothing happened for a moment. Then one of the street Arabs stepped forward and shouted something. His voice echoed in shrill, urgent notes in the narrow alley.

"Can't you—" Naomi began.

"Israeli!" the leader of the Arabs cried. "Kill the spy!"

Something struck her in the back. She staggered, almost fell, and Ta'arife helped her up. He had shoved her. He laughed silently.

"Run!" he cried.

For an instant she stood without understanding. The breath was squeezed from her lungs. She felt the pain of Ta'arife's sudden blow, like a numbness.

"Run!" he shouted again. "That way!"

The Arabs walked toward them, then trotted. They began to yell. Naomi stood frozen in the shadowy alley. Ta'arife was pointing to a narrow slot between two nearby buildings. He gave an impatient exclamation, drew his gun, and pushed her again.

Without thinking, she began to run.

The moment she moved, the Arabs sprinted after her. Their yells and cries sounded almost at her heels. Without understanding, with no knowledge of how she was being used, or why, Naomi began to run.

And nightmare turned into reality.

It was all carefully arranged. Ta'arife's men did their work well.

The city was coming awake to violence again. The sun was over the horizon of the sea. Its first rays touched the houses and streets of Jidrat with searing heat. Far in the distance, a grenade exploded, like the opening note of a devil's symphony. The faraway thump echoed in the air for a moment; then a chord was struck by a series of mortar shells. Smoke plumed into the sky from the gardens of Faiz. A machine gun chattered, adding its staccato notes to the growing series of discords. And, like a sleeping giant, the people and the mob appeared again; first in ones and twos, then in small armed groups eager for more burning and killing and looting. The sound of the mob began as a low, rumbling growl. Here and there came a shrill cry, a shriek of pain, a shout of triumph. Fires broke out here, there—in half a dozen places. The city shook itself and awoke once again, with a roar, to rebellion.

Colonel Ta'arife counted on his fox hunt to bring final success today.

Naomi's first thought was to get back to the Hotel al-Zaysir somehow. Other Europeans were there. People who might help, who might demand civilized protection for her or at least be witnesses to what was being done to her. She did not think about it too clearly.

But the alleyway into which Ta'arife had pushed her twisted away from the sanctuary of the hotel. When she came to the end of it, she stood blinded by the sudden glare of sunlight on a small bazaar. All the shops were closed, the baradas empty. Nobody was in sight. She looked behind her. The band of street Arabs trotted a short distance to the rear. When they saw her looking at them, they paused, too.

"Kill the spy!" one of them shouted. "Kill!"

The cry started her running again. She tried to turn right, racing across the uneven pavement of the square, still trying to circle back to the al-Zaysir. But as if they had suddenly sprung from the earth, another band of Arabs appeared in the street entrance she had chosen.

She checked her headlong flight, gasping.

The heat of the sun struck her. Turning, she ran the other way.

Now they closed the gap. Very slightly. She ran faster, up one street, down another. Panic rode on her back. She stumbled and fell sprawling in the filth of the gutter. A Moslem woman came out of the dark hole of a doorway and saw her on her hands and knees. The woman, veiled below the eyes, looked at the men who chased her and heard their screams. Her eyes widened. She spit at Naomi and clutched at her, trying to hold her down. Naomi screamed and clubbed at her with her handbag and scratched at the veil and staggered up again. The woman shrilled curses after her as she ran.

The harbor, she thought. The quay and the ship.

MacPherson would do something for her.

Oh God, help me! she prayed.

She turned left, toward the harbor. More people chased her now: a growing crowd, an organism that grew and fattened on her terrified flight. Miraculously, the street ahead was empty. She saw the distant glare of water in the harbor —a glimpse snatched between two coral-block buildings. She ran harder. The breath burned in her lungs.

She stumbled and fell again.

Her dress was torn. When she got up, she couldn't find her handbag and the gun. Oh God. Where had she lost it? How had it happened? Wildly, she looked behind her. She would use the gun, if she had it now. On herself, if necessary. Yes, on herself. That would be best.

But she couldn't see the gun or the leather bag. A running mass of men in flapping, dirty robes turned the corner and saw her and shrieked in triumph. She turned and ran.

Her left leg hurt. She had scraped it painfully on the cobblestones when she fell. Fortunately, her shoes were sensible flats, strapped snugly up to her ankles.

She went down another street, and saw another group of six men suddenly block her way to the harbor.

How did that happen? she wondered. She was trapped. She was being driven this way and that, like a hunted animal.

It was a nightmare.

She ran and fell and ran again. The streets slanted upward, going away from the harbor, away from the hotel. Higher and higher into the city by a series of stone stairways in the alleys and streets. The streets, yes! She had to get off the streets. Hide. Where? Somewhere. Where? Anywhere! Hide!

She looked for an open door, an entrance, anything. The mob howled and stormed after her. Strange that they couldn't run as fast as she. No matter. Keep running! Look for a place to hide!

Where?

She was alone in a city thirsting for her blood. Running, falling, running. Her hands were bleeding. Her skirt was torn.

The breath tore through her throat, threatened to rupture her lungs. There was a pain in her chest, a clutching and squeezing that threatened her with a bursting heart.

She saw the open doorway.

She ran into it.

Darkness blinded her. Green globes danced and whirled before her eyes. She could see nothing. She felt stairs, smelled urine and human excrement and the stale odor of roasted lamb. She looked up the stairway. A man stood there. He was tall, enormous. A knife gleamed in his hands. He looked uncertain: his bullet-like head, shaven and unnatural, cocked to one side as he listened to the shrieking mob not far away.

"Help me," she moaned. She did not know she spoke in Hungarian. "Help me, please. . . ."

The man answered in Arabic, querulously. She did not understand him. But she understood his smile. He started down the steps for her, the knife lifted.

She screamed and stumbled back and ran out into the hot, bright street again.

How long had she been running? There was firing up ahead. Through the beat of blood in her ears, she distinguished the crackling of rifles, the tat-a-tat of a light machine gun, the thud and thump of mortars. She ran past a group of khaki-clad soldiers who yelled at her and stared in wonder and then turned incredulously to the mob at her heels. One of the soldiers reached from behind his sandbag parapet and clutched at her arm. She spun away, fell. Her dress was torn even more. She saw the soldier's face—young, astonished, puzzled. He was part of a regular platoon, a squad wearing the black armbands of rebellion—the Q'adi's men, or Ta'arife's, assaulting the walls of the palace.

The walls were straight ahead.

She saw a wide, bright, sunlit square; a broad avenue that led to soaring medieval battlements. The ponderous gates to the entrance were closed. Return fire crackled from the walls where the Imam's guards still stood, fearful and uncertain of what this second day of battle would bring.

There was nowhere else to go. She ran toward the closed gate.

A bullet spanked the mosaic tile pavement of the square beside her flying feet. She looked back again.

The mob saw her fleeing toward the sanctuary of the square that faced the Bab es-Salam, the main gate by which the palace, Faiz, could be breached. The mob was an irresistable flood. Yesterday's dead who had fallen in the square trying to assault the gates were forgotten in the bloodlust whipped up by the chase, so carefully controlled by Ta'arife's men who had driven her here where the tide of the maddened crowd could not be stopped.

The mob saw her fleeing toward the sanctuary of the Imam's palace. She stood between two forces—a tiny figure in torn white, her dark hair streaming, her face smeared and dirty, her eyes blurred by sweat and fear. Unwittingly, she had led the howling men straight to the towering gates.

The Imam's guards on the walls saw her and saw the mob. Yesterday had not been like this. This was a human flood, howling for blood.

They threw down their weapons and scrambled away from the wall.

Naomi came to the gate, and turned.

It was closed against her.

She faced the mob, then, and saw their faces, across the broad square with its shattered palm trees and broken houses.

She could run no further. There was no other place to go.

Let them kill me now, she thought.

Let them do it quickly.

Chapter Eighteen

KOLIA MIKELNIKOV saw her.

He was awake at dawn and had gone down to the bar of the al-Zaysir for breakfast wearing a light gray summer suit and a straw Panama that covered his short gray-tinged hair. His long, sad face was expressionless as he joined the other Europeans at the makeshift meal. They knew he was Russian. He did not know how they had learned this, but he supposed the soldiers had talked. It made no difference—except that the other Europeans, in their common trouble, did not speak to him or even nod. Their faces showed signs of strain, and they all stopped talking when Mikelnikov arrived.

They look at me as if I were a leper in the streets of Jidrat, he thought. They blame me for all that has happened here.

But this was only partly the truth.

Afterward, he was picked up by Colonel Ta'arife, who seemed to be in a particularly jovial and optimistic mood. The assault on Faiz would begin in a very few minutes. They could view it from the roof of one of the buildings fronting Faiz Square and the Bab es-Salam. It would be interesting. The Major had fought in World War II with the Soviet forces, of course; he had been in Stalingrad; thus he would appreciate the street fighting, the method chosen to crash the gates.

There would be heavy losses in a frontal attack, Kolia suggested. Would the rebel troops have the courage to charge across the square?

Oh, they would be screened, Ta'arife said airily. The people themselves would lead the attack.

They had gone to one of the buildings on Faiz Square and stood on the roof, waiting. The sun struck the back of Kolia Mikelnikov's neck like a hammer blow. They were sheltered here, standing behind a parapet on the rooftop three floors above the broad, barren square, from sniper fire coming from the walls of Faiz. Smoke rolled across the city from the new fires set by the mob. It smelled like the smoke of a burning garbage dump, Kolia thought.

When Naomi first appeared, running out of a side street to the broad, open reach of the sunlit square, he did not recognize her.

He had put her out of his thoughts, with the end of night.

He cocked an eyebrow at Ta'arife, for an explanation, when he saw the mob pouring from the street, after the running girl.

"It is an Israeli spy," Ta'arife said pleasantly. "I set the people to chivvy her this way. Nothing will stop them now. They are maddened with their blood lust. No bullets from Faiz will stop them until they have gone through and over the wall after her."

Kolia did not recognize Naomi until she turned at the tall, high barrier of the Bab es-Salam and faced the mob streaming toward her, and waited for death.

She had been given a good start. The square was over a hundred yards across, and she had reached the gates of Faiz before the mob really started pouring into sight like an angry river of open-mouthed, screaming faces.

A machine gun chattered and the tide of humanity paused for an instant.

And he recognized her.

He saw her face clearly from the parapet. Saw the stark, white terror that shaped her mouth, her enormous eyes. Saw her torn clothing, the dirt and filth on her where she had stumbled and fallen in the streets. Saw her as a hunted animal deliberately set loose to lead the pack of murderous hounds to where their master wanted them to go.

And their master, Colonel Ta'arife, was saying, "This girl, this Naomi Haledi, came from—"

Kolia did not stop to think, to question, to doubt the possibility of what he saw. He had been trained and conditioned through long years in the MVD to expect only the unexpected. He raised his voice in a mighty shout that was torn abruptly from his lungs.

"Naomi!"

The girl stood with her arms spread wide, her back flat against the tall gate that had trapped her. Her face turned in the direction of his voice. She could not see him from where he stood on the roof of the nearby building. But her mouth was open and he saw the lift and break of her breathing, saw the shine of fear in her eyes. . . .

The crowd had halted.

"Stop them," Mikelnikov said. He did not recognize the sound of his own voice. "Stop them, Colonel."

"But I do not understand. . . ."

They were alone on the roof. Kolia drew his Tokarev.

Ta'arife saw the gun in the Russian's hand, but he was only puzzled.

"You did this? You arranged this?"

"Of course. It was clever. If the crowd can be moved forward now—"

Kolia shot him.

He shot to kill, and the bullet smashed into Ta'arife's chest just an inch to the left of the sternum, the breastbone, under the neatly pressed lapel of the khaki shirt that carried three rows of campaign ribbons and medals that Ta'arife, for the most part, had bestowed upon himself. The bullet smashed its way through Ta'arife's heart and lungs and came out just beneath his shoulder blade.

And Ta'arife was dead before he hit the floor.

Kolia ran. There were other men on the roof now; aides and officers who had joined the clique of the rebellion. They were too stunned to interfere. Kolia found the stairs by which they had ascended and started to leap down, his long legs trembling, and he stumbled and fell part of the way and forced himself to take the second flight a little more carefully.

He kept the Tokarev in his hand.

When he burst out of the building into the square, Ta'arife's paid agitators in the crowd—who had done so well their job of herding the girl this way, like hounds chasing a rabbit—paid no attention to the single shot they heard or to the sudden clamor of officers' shrill voices from the rooftop.

They knew their job and they did it.

They screeched for blood, and the mob, with a mighty howl, surged forward across the square toward the lone, small figure of the girl pressed against the heavy barrier of the Gate of Peace.

That was when the Imam's troops threw away their guns, knowing that defense was useless, and fled.

Kolia burst into the sunlit square and found himself in a small, running knot of wild-eyed men. He drove his way through them like a bull—grateful for his massive, strong body—and broke out ahead of them.

He ran toward Naomi, shouting her name.

He saw her face turn toward him in disbelief. He saw her eyes widen, her mouth quiver, and he saw his name on her lips, but he could not hear her cry because the howl of the mob was thunderous behind him.

He reached her only a moment before the surging torrent of people crossed Faiz Square.

He had time only to throw himself beside her, to put one long, great arm around her and raise the gun toward the crowd.

It was hopeless.

He saw their faces and knew that nothing, nothing at all, —not threats, nor death itself—could stop the tide of screaming humanity that came for them.

And then, miraculously, the Bab es-Salam opened ponderously behind them.

The Imam Yazid had said his morning prayers with the first glimpse of the sun as it rose above the sea. It was difficult for his old joints to accommodate the kneeling posture required on his prayer rug as he faced north and west, toward Mecca and the holy stone of Kaaba. He said his prayers slowly, savoring the meaning of the phrases, the devotion and the submission demanded, and added a prayer that those who were his enemies would relent and dwell al yemen—at the right hand, the lucky side—of Allah forever.

Faiz was empty.

The servants were gone, both those who were loyal, and those who took bribes. The guard was gone, too, and only a few of his personal troops still held their stations on the palace wall that faced Faiz Square below. Well, no matter. He knew what must be done this day. He was an old man and he had lived for many years. Perhaps too many.

He heard the growing, growling thunder of the people who crowded close to the Bab es-Salam and he walked slowly, dressed in his white robe; a patriarch who might have walked in just this way in just this dress in the time of the Prophet himself. He looked once at his sleeping chamber, at the books of poetry and philosophy and history—all these that contained the best and most glorious of Islam—and he said goodbye to them, individually and all at once, knowing them all and knowing that the books with their rich leather bindings that he had treasured were not important in themselves, but only in what they engraved on the hearts of men.

He took only the Koran with him, holding the heavy tome to his thin breast.

The long avenue, with its terra cotta lions and paving blocks of marble, was shaded under the palms. Here and there, on the green watered gardens, were the scars of mortar shells. But it was nothing. Nothing. He was grateful for whatever shade still remained as he walked down the hill, toward the gate, toward the city of his people.

It was too late for anything else, he thought.

Too late for so many things.

He heard a single shot from somewhere above the roofs of the buildings that formed three sides of Faiz Square. He paid no attention to it. There had been many shots lately. The fourth side of the square was the wall of the palace, and in the wall was the Gate of Peace, the Bab es-Salam. On the other side of the city there was another Gate of Peace, part of the old wall that had been built when the Portuguese came four hundred years ago. That was after Islam had reached its height, been thrown back in the West, turned on itself in schism and decadence, and slowly dissolved into emptiness and dreams of a Mahdi who would come and save everyone.

There was no salvation, the old man thought quietly, except within each man's individual soul.

No outside force could help. By the grace and the wisdom of Allah, each man had to help himself.

He saw the soldiers, the last of his guards, running from the wall, thrashing through the shrubbery. Oleanders grew thickly among choice specimen trees, among olive and lemon and pomegranates that made a miniature, carefully planned jungle just inside the Bab es-Salam.

The gate was closed, but outside he heard the cries of his people.

The mechanism operated electrically and power, coming from Faiz's separate generator, fed the levers that opened the gate. The Imam Yazid pushed a button in the sentry box— deserted, now—and stepped back and watched the gates swing wide.

He stood alone in the wide avenue. He saw a foreign man and a foreign woman turn and gape, staring as if at a miracle. The man and the woman turned and dashed into the palace grounds and ran out of sight into the oleander shrubbery nearby.

He did not look at them twice.

He saw the mob like a giant wave, a single convulsive torrent, a sea of faces pouring toward him. The faces had only one mouth. They screamed with hate.

For a moment, the old man's heart lurched within him. Then he held the heavy Koran closer to his breast, in his left hand, and held up his right hand.

"Children!" he called.

The mob came to a halt. There was silence.

"My children!" the Imam called.

There was at the head of the mob a man who had been promised one hundred silver rupees from Colonel Ta'arife if the day was successful. He was the best agitator, the smartest street orator of them all. He was anxious to get the money. He didn't know that Ta'arife was dead.

He screamed, "Kill the Englisi!"

He cried, "Kill the foreign imperialists!"

He shrieked, "Kill the Israeli spy that the Imam harbors and takes in as his friend!"

The Imam did not understand the shrill words. He saw the crowd start forward: shouting, pushing, yelling in triumph because the gate was open at last, the fighting was over, the palace lay open to them, waiting for their looting hands.

They crowded forward; ran, pushed, shoved. Those who fell were trampled underfoot. Some were squeezed to death against the walls of the Gate of Peace as the mob tried to funnel through the opening.

The Iman felt something strike his brow. It was a stone someone had thrown. He wavered, feeling the light of day fade momentarily from his eyes. His face was wet. He touched it with his fingers and saw how old and gnarled and brown his hand was—the hand of an old man. It was curious, he thought, how bright and red the blood of an old man can be.

The crowd threw itself upon him. First they used fists and stones and even their teeth. Then came the knives. The Imam tried to hold on to his Koran. He did not want to have it trampled in the dust under so many bare feet. He felt pain, and a darkness came. He saw flicks of light through the darkness, and the flicks were the knives.

They slashed at the old man's body and dismembered him. The amount of blood was surprising. They disemboweled him and tried to hack off his head, but this failed, and then someone threw a rope over the top of the Bab es-Salam and someone else tied the other end of the rope to the stump of a leg and a third man hoisted with a will and the body of the Imam Yazid al-Maari went swinging high above their heads, his white robe flapping—now white, now red—his partly severed head like a clot of torn flesh dangling from his torso. His robe fell off and he hung there, swaying, old and withered and skeletal, naked to the hot sun that shone upon Jidrat.

Chapter Nineteen

FAIZ was built upon a high, flat hill overlooking the city. Its walls were erected by the Imam Zamil Sayid al-Maari in the sixteenth century, with the help of the Portuguese who held the imamate in conquest. Portuguese engineers had laid out the fortifications, with special stress on the frontage that faced the city. They also built Faiz Square and arranged for the lines of fire from the Bab es-Salam. On all other sides of the hill were sheer basaltic cliffs that offered no line of attack, although here and there smaller gates pierced the walls and an occasional goat trail slanted up the steep walls of rock. In one place in the rear, opposite the main gate, the palace itself formed part of the defense battlements built on the very edge of the precipice. A trail led up to this gate, too. It was a position impossible to assault and, therefore, guarded only perfunctorily. It was this goat trail and this gate that Durell, Amr, and Zoraya used to gain entrance to Faiz.

They had walked less than an hour at dawn through the Djebel Haradh foothills, and then they came to the highway leading to the oil fields.

Durell had listened to Esme Kenton's story with quiet solicitude. He knew, now, the answer to John Blaney's death. One of the Q'adi Ghezri's nameless assassins had done the job, and Blaney's file could be closed. He heard Esme tell about Tabib, her servant, who must have stumbled upon Messaoud at Ain Gemilha and been attacked and had his tongue cut out, and who had gone running, crazed, into the fatal heat of the desert.

When the Englishwoman finished talking, he said, "Do you think you can walk with us back to Jidrat?"

"Yes. I am quite all right."

"Are you sure? We could get help—"

"I'll go with you," Esme said.

He saw that her quiet strength would sustain her. She did not speak again about her husband or what had happened to her in the cave.

The sun was above the horizon when they reached the

highway. The sun's glare hammered at their unprotected bodies. The road was a ribbon of concrete curving out of the city toward the oil fields where the American and British oil engineers had holed up for the duration of the rebellion.

Luck was with them. They hadn't been on the road five minutes before two jeeps came along, carrying four men. They were Americans. Durell signalled them, aware that their small party was eyed with incredulous wonder by the Americans. They told him that their orders were to stay out of the city. They thought Durell mad when he asked to borrow one of the jeeps. They handed out cigarettes and two cans of C-rations and a thermos of coffee for their breakfast. Esme ate quietly while Durell dickered for the jeep. Amr said nothing— squatting in the shade of one of the vehicles, his eyes indrawn and remote, detached from what was happening. The welts on his back where he had been whipped by the Al Murra tribes-men were painful; the scars on his soul were less obvious, but they showed in his eyes.

Durell borrowed a loaded Colt .45 from one of the engi-neers, who looked at him as if he were already a dead man. He ordered Esme back to the camp in the oil field with the Americans. She objected, but finally she rode off with them, crowding into their remaining vehicle.

In the jeep, it was only a short run to the outskirts of Jidrat. The few houses and streets they passed were empty, blasted by the cruel sun. Nobody stopped them. In a few minutes, Durell, at Zoraya's direction, stopped the car at the foot of the goat path that climbed the black-rock face of the hill where Faiz loomed.

They heard the mob, like distant thunder, at the palace gates half a mile around the hill. But nothing stirred on the old Portuguese battlements and palace walls high above.

Amr spoke for the first time, in a curiously flat voice.

"What do you want of me, Cajun?"

"We're going up there to help your grandfather."

"It is useless."

"We won't know that until we try."

"You saw how the Al Murra treated me. How can I forget it? You lead me only to my death."

Durell said, "The Al Murra were always sworn enemies of your family. The oath of allegiance they took was not meant to be respected."

"They whipped me like a slave. Like an animal."

"You asked for it," Durell said bluntly. "It could have been worse. I know you blame me for bringing you here. But are you really afraid to die?"

"I don't know," Amr said.

"Your grandfather is not afraid. Are you weaker than an old man?"

Amr's head jerked up and his flat, dark eyes reacted for the first time. "Yazid is a kind, gentle old man. He does not know what monsters stir the world these days. His is the courage of ignorance."

"I think not. You know better, too."

Amr stood up. He looked up at the towering basalt cliff and the palace walls above. The muted roar of the crowd, hidden on the other side of the hill in Faiz Square, sounded momentarily louder as a trick of the wind brought the noise to them. He shuddered. His round face had taken on a pale, gaunt look in the past twenty-four hours, as if the desert sun of his homeland had bleached the flesh on his fox bones. His mouth drooped. He looked unpredictable and unknowable, and Durell wondered if he would ever understand the Arab.

"Let me be," Amr said. "I will go with you."

Together, they climbed the path to the wall. There was a small gateway in the wall, with an empty sentry box. The gate stood open, the way the fleeing guard had left it. As they pushed through they became aware of a sudden silence from the crowd attacking the other side of the palace grounds. They did not know that at this moment the Imam Yazid had opened the Bab es-Salam to his children.

Zoraya said, "Why is no one here? Where have they gone?"

The tiled floors of the palace rooms echoed hollowly under their heels. Amr led the way. They saw no one. They were not challenged.

They passed through ornate dining halls that could seat hundreds at banquets—and in the past, often had—and then walked through an open garden of fruit trees. Durell carried his borrowed Colt .45 in his hand. Amr walked faster. In the cool inner chambers, the sun's fury did not penetrate. Amr ran up a staircase and down a wide corridor to the front of the building.

Now the fury of the mob burst into full sound again. They heard incredibly inhuman things being called out by the crowd. Amr's face was pale.

"Yazid!" he called. "Grandfather!"

They followed at Amr's heels into the old man's sleeping

chamber. His books and narghile looked peaceful, untouched. No servant was in sight. There was a balcony beyond a tall, carved Indian screen. Amr halted, breathing hard. A sheen of sweat covered his face.

"What are they screaming, out there? It must be over. The guards have deserted. Why haven't they come to loot and burn?" He turned haunted eyes to Durell. "You see, we have lost! Ta'arife wins today. In a few minutes they will come in here and kill us."

Durell had gone to the balcony. His voice sounded strange in his ears when he spoke. "Look out there," he said.

"Where?"

"At the gate. Your grandfather tried to stop them."

Amr's eyes searched Durell's face. He drew a deep breath. "I don't want to look. I want—" He glanced at Zoraya. "I don't know what I want. Why did you bring me back here?" he cried suddenly.

His words went winging through the empty palace that lay under the heel of the sun's march in the morning sky.

"Look at your grandfather," Durell said harshly.

Slowly, reluctantly, Amr went to the balcony and stared at the Bab es-Salam. His face went empty, grew quiet. One hand held onto the screen. He looked small and shrunken. Durell did not speak again. Zoraya looked at the long sweep of palace lawns, at the formal gardens and hedges, the ornamental trees, the massed shrubbery artfully arranged beside the wide marble avenue that swept up from the massive old gate. She saw the gate was open. She saw the mob that coagulated around it, and then she saw the naked torso of the Imam Yazid hanging by the stump of one leg from the end of the rope that had been thrown over the battlement. She made a small sound, nothing more. Her enormous amber eyes moved quickly to Durell and then back to Amr. She stood beside the prince.

"He was alone," she whispered. "He tried to stop them."

Amr's voice was a wrench of agony. 'Yes. And look . . . look what they did to him."

"Go down there," Durell said sharply.

"What?"

"Can you do less than the old man tried to do?"

But Amr did not seem to hear. He sank slowly to his knees, and his eyes looked at something that Durell would never see.

He did not at first understand the words that Amr addressed

to himself as he looked at the hooting mob and the swinging body of his grandfather above the Bab es-Salam.

And then they came clearly to Durell.

It was an old medieval prayer.

"O Thou, than whom there is no other lord to be worshipped, and no other diety to be looked to, beyond whom there is no other creator to be feared, and no vizier to be influenced, and no chamberlain to be bribed—" The words blurred for a moment in Amr's throat, then came clearly again. "There is no god but God, and Mohammed is his prophet."

Amr stood up and looked at Durell. He smiled strangely.

"Once I told you, my friend, that I was never able to say this with full belief. But I have said it now, for the first time, with full understanding and absolute acceptance." He paused. "Will you come with me?"

"Yes."

"And you, Zoraya?"

She looked at him with wide, tawny eyes, "Yes, Amr. I will always stand with you. Do you truly want me?"

"Yes. I truly do."

"Then I will go with you, too."

Often, much later, Durell thought of what followed and tried to understand it. But, later, it was difficult to recapture that morning on the shore of Arabia, facing the burning sea and the flaming city. He could recall the faces of the mob, the inflamed passions that struck the prince, Zoraya, and him like the blast of a furnace when they walked down the broad avenue from Faiz to the Bab es-Salam. He would always see the distorted faces of the mob in his mind, see them jumping and dancing like puppets reacting to strings of hate. Here and there among the faces that squeezed through the gate was one that reflected awe and fear and perhaps shame, but it was difficult to remember this last very clearly.

He felt his own fear in him as he walked through the hot sunlight, toward the crowd that turned in startled wonder at the sight of their three small figures. They walked on, facing the inflamed wrath of the city.

He was not ashamed of his fear. Only a fool would react otherwise. But he walked beside Amr, with the girl between them, and then Amr halted them and walked on alone, a little ahead.

The crowd fell silent.

They turned in astonishment toward the Prince of Jidrat.

A man cried Amr's name, and it rolled back and forth through the blood-spattered mob like a wave, growing as it reached those in the back, still jammed in Faiz Square.

The name came back to them in a shout.

And then silence returned.

Amr's words fell into the silence like stones into a dark pool.

His Arabic was quiet, gutteral, forceful. He was transformed. He stood straighter and taller, an image of his old royal self. But there was no petty anger in his voice. His words were hard and forceful.

He told the crowd to go home.

He said he had come back to assume the imamate for himself. He told them he would never leave Jidrat again.

He told them he would bring peace and dignity to Jidrat once more, when the shame of their crimes had been eased by the passage of time.

It was almost enough.

But not quite.

Ta'arife's paid agitators did not know their master was dead. The man who had thrown the first stone at the old Imam decided that where the tactic had succeeded once it would succeed again. He scooped up a stone from the rubble at the gate and straightened to throw it.

Durell shot him.

It had to be a true shot, sharp and clean and accurate. If it missed or only wounded, the mob would be galvanized into bloody life again.

The heavy report of his borrowed Colt .45 was like a massive punctuation mark to Prince Amr's speech.

The agitator fell without a sound.

"Go home," Amr said quietly. "Go to your homes now."

Everything hung in the balance.

Leaderless, not knowing Ta'arife was dead, the street crowd and the soldiers of the mutiny had no one to spur them on. Those in the van under the gate pressed back. A murmuring arose. There was a disorganized pushing and shoving. The crowd gave way. An aisle was formed.

Through the aisle came a man in black riding a white donkey. It was the Q'adi Ghezri.

He looked not to right or left as he rode toward Amr al-

Maari. When he was a short distance away, under the bloody remainder of the Imam's body, he dismounted from the donkey. His black robe swept the dust. The green band of his turban, which indicated he had fulfilled the holy requirement of a hadj to Mecca, shone under the hot sun.

His face was the face of a beaten eagle.

He stood in the sunlight before Prince Amr and said: "I have learned that Colonel Ta'arife is dead. My people are disorganized."

"And your weapons have been blown up," Amr said curtly.

"Yes. A messenger has also told me this."

Amr said to the tall, black-robed figure, "You are under arrest for treason."

The Q'adi bowed. In his eyes was an acceptance of fate, a submission to events that moved beyond the powers of men.

"It is as Allah wills," he said.

And the people went home.

Chapter Twenty

THE REVOLUTION ended like a balloon burst by a pin. But Major Kolia Mikelnikov still had a job to do. He had his gun, and there was Durell. Not even Naomi had made him forget. The habits of discipline were too strongly ingrained in him to do otherwise.

Naomi was a miracle. And so was the fact they were both still alive. The Imam had saved them. His appearance at the gate, the pause he gave the onrushing crowd, and then the distraction of the mob as they killed him and hanged his remains from the Bab es-Salam gave Kolia and Naomi a chance to hide in the thick oleander shrubbery on the Faiz grounds.

There was no time for words then. They witnessed everything from their hiding place. Several times the trampling feet of the mob came so close they were visible to them through the dense green foliage. The shrill cries of the Jidrattis echoed all around and above them.

Kolia was prepared to die. He could not question Naomi as to how she had appeared out of nowhere in this place where he had not even thought of looking for her. He knew now that she was the Israeli girl that Ta'arife had planned to use as a lure to inflame the mob into a last assault on Faiz, and he silently cursed his inattention, knowing now that Naomi had been in the al-Zaysir with him, so near and unsuspected, living out her hours of terror.

How could she ever forgive him? How—when he could not forgive himself?

In those moments when Naomi shuddered beside him as they lay hidden in the bushes, with death from the mob so near, he felt that this miracle was too great to accept. It was a trick of fate, he thought, and any moment they would be found and he would empty the Tokarev at the nearest men, and then it would all end, before it could begin again.

He did not do more than whisper Naomi's name and smile encouragingly into her wide eyes.

Then Amr appeared, and Mikelnikov witnessed what followed.

171

He could have shot Durell then.

But the thought of what might follow, the new lease he would give to mob violence and the immediate danger to Naomi, made him put his gun down again.

Still, he did not forget his mission.

It was long minutes before they felt safe. Once Naomi started to rise, but he pulled her back into their leafy hiding place. Naomi stared at him in utter wonderment. He sensed confusion, a struggle in her. He touched her bruised cheek gently with his big, strong hand; he covered her breast with a torn shred of her dress. She seemed unaware of it.

"Kolia?" she whispered. "It is really you?"

"Yes. It is something to wonder at, is it not?"

"But where did you come from?"

He told her, briefly. "And you?"

She told him how she came to Jidrat aboard the *Atlantic Maid*. How she had fled Budapest to run and hide and reach Vienna, and how from Vienna she had gone to Rome with other refugees, and at last had arrived in Haifa.

"I have an apartment now in Tel Aviv," she said. The words meant nothing, simply filling the space of distance and time between them. "Tel Aviv is a beautiful city. I have a good job. I was happy there."

"I see. Will you go back?"

She remembered her terror. "Will the Jidrattis let me?"

"I think it can be arranged now."

She said: "Well, then, if I can, I will go back to Tel Aviv."

"Naomi—?'"

"No," she said.

"Will you never forgive me?"

"How can I?"

"If you hadn't run away, I could have helped. I searched everywhere, in so many cities, looking at every woman with black hair and the shape of your body, and every time I was disappointed I died a little."

"Perhaps it was better that way."

"Look at me, Naomi."

She looked at him. Her eyes were blank. But her mouth trembled. He said, "Are we still married, Naomi?"

"I suppose so. Legally, yes."

"So you are still my wife."

"I am nothing to you."

"Your father and your brothers—"

"I try not to think of it any more."

"Do you hate me so much, then?"

"I don't hate you. Last night, when I thought I would never be alive at this hour, I stopped hating you, Kolia. I only wanted to remember how it once was, how wonderful you were to me, how we loved each other."

"I still love you," he said.

"You killed them," she said, meaning her father and brothers.

He said nothing. He could not excuse himself on the basis of duty or military necessity or the need to preserve oneself by following orders. He could not tell her how he had protested against General Murov's plans. Nothing could help him.

"So it is finished?" he whispered.

"You do not understand. I have forgiven you," she said. "But it means nothing. Have you changed? Would you not do it again, if you had to? Isn't that right?"

"I don't know." His face was long and sad and heavy in the shadows of the sheltering oleanders. He thought of Durell, of his job here. Where did it end? Where did the machine and the state leave off, and where did the man begin? "I don't know," he said again.

And then Durell walked alone down the empty avenue to the Bab es-Salam. He walked slowly, his hands at his sides. He was looking for them. He had heard about the Israeli girl and the Russian who had vanished when the Imam opened the gate.

Mikelnikov knew that Durell wanted him.

He stood up with the Tokarev in his hand.

"Durell!" he called.

Durell saw him. His hands were at his sides. He was covered by Kolia's gun. His face was expressionless in the glare of sunlight.

"Kolia," Naomi said. "What are you doing?"

"Be still, little one. It is between me and this man."

"But he saved us, Kolia! Why do you have your gun—?"

"I have my job to do," Mikelnikov said, and the words were tortured in his throat. "Do you understand how it is? If I fail, I can never go home!"

"Yes, or they will kill you," Durell said. "The people you work for sometimes are like that. And you are anxious to stay with them?"

"Yes, I don't want to be alone and homeless like—like—"
He stared at Naomi.

Naomi suddenly wrenched free and tore through the shrubbery and stood beside the American. Her face was white; her eyes blazed.

"Then kill us both," she said. "That is what you are good for, Kolia. I was alone and homeless, too. So kill me, like you killed my father and my brothers!" Mikelnikov stared at her. His big body, strong and full of life, was devoted to the duty he had been trained for.

Durell waited. He knew it was useless to try for his own gun. He did not understand what was happening between the Russian and the Israeli girl. He stood in the hot sunlight and wondered.

"Naomi?" Kolia whispered. "I can never go back if I—"

"Back to what?" she asked.

"I—I don't know."

"If you love me, Kolia, will you come with me?"

"With you?"

"To my new home. To my apartment in Tel Aviv."

He said, "They would not want me. Or accept me."

"Yes, they will. Yes! I want you. So they will want you."

Major Kolia Mikelnikov stood on a threshold. He could step either way. He looked at Naomi and Durell and saw they were not afraid. He saw the look in her eyes. It was one of hoping and praying. But not for herself. She was praying for him. For him, and perhaps a new life. If he stepped forward, he could never go back. He would have to live with her people then, forever. He wondered if that would be so bad. Theirs was a new, hard, pioneering world; and they were strangers; but they were not complete strangers, because they were Naomi's people. He could make himself useful, he thought. He was strong and intelligent and he could work at many constructive things. He could build a new life and a new way for so many others who were like Naomi.

He felt a stir of excitement in him and laughed. He threw down the gun. It lay in the dust and the debris of the Gate of Peace.

Durell stooped to pick it up.

"Leave it there," Kolia said. "I am finished with it."

"I wish I could," Durell said. "I wish I could go with you."

By evening, the city was quiet again. The fires were out.

The bazaars were open, the shops unshuttered, and the merchants sat on their *baradas* and drank hot sweet tea and bargained for their wares.

At the Faiz Palace, the servants had returned and the guards paraded at drill, imitating the rigid British steps of the Buckingham Palace Guard, in unconscious obedience to their English Army instructors of another year.

The oil wells were pumping again. The tankers at the quay were like strange sea monsters, sinking low in the water as they sucked the oil into their bellies. The sun went down behind the Djebel Haradh, and a cool wind blew from the sea.

Durell remembered that the nakhoda had called the wind the breath of God.

The wind blew quietly through Faiz, and into the room where he sat drinking coffee with Amr and Zoraya. From the east side of the city came the sound of the first plane lifting from the reopened airport; the big silver jet circled Jidrat once and then flew west.

"You understand," Amr said, "I thought it wise to get the Russian and his wife out of Jidrat as soon as possible. I decided it was best to let them board the plane."

"Are they still in love?" Zoraya asked.

"Yes," Durell said.

Amr said briskly, "As for you, my friend, I give you my personal thanks, but nothing more. Do you understand? I promise you and your government nothing. No special favors, no special arrangements. Jidrat will be neutral."

"Like Egypt?" Durell asked wryly.

"Truly neutral. What happened here was not an affliction brought in from the outside, like a disease. No, the disease is here, in the fact that we have much to learn and do and change, before we can walk with the rest of the world. I can help them. I shall spend the rest of my life helping them. And the past shall be only a dream."

"No one could ask for more than fairness and justice to all, Imam Amr," Durell said gravely. He looked at Zoraya. "And you?"

She said nothing.

Amr said, "She is my wife. She stays at my side."

"It is the will of Allah," Durell said.

The cool soothing breeze of evening blew through the broken window of the U. S. Consulate office. T. P. Fenner finished talking on the radio-telephone through a hookup via Karachi. He had given a long report on the abortive revolution in Jidrat. He had talked long and earnestly and persuasively, and the return message had filled him with an enormous sense of gratification.

First, he was commended highly for the job he had done here during the past forty-eight hours. As a result, he was directed to call upon the new Imam as soon as it was convenient, with full credentials and immediate recognition of the new regime. When this was done, he was to await his successor, who was on his way from Malaya to relieve him.

T. P. Fenner was being promoted.

His next post was in the Paris Embassy.

He sighed, quite contented with himself, and reached for the bottle of bourbon on his desk. Then he chuckled. In Paris, he would have to develop a taste for fine old brandies, he decided. There could be worse duties, he thought.

Yes, he felt quite satisfied with T. P. Fenner. The report he had telephoned may have been somewhat colored, but he already believed his version of what had happened. And who could prove what had happened here in this crazy city last night. Nobody. He was here at the consulate, and all was quiet again.

No damage done.

And he had his promotion.

All good things, he decided, came to those who wait.